# THE PRISONERS
# OF QUAI DONG

# THE

# OF QUAI

# PRISONERS

# DONG

### by Victor Kolpacoff

THE NEW AMERICAN LIBRARY

*FOR LANE*
*AND CAROL TOLER*

# THE PRISONERS
# OF QUAI DONG

CHAPTER *ONE*

O U R  D A Y in the military stockade at Quai Dong began at five o'clock in the morning, when the bass voice of the
loudspeaker ordered us to form our line for breakfast. Or, to
be more exact, it began at half past four. That was when the
glare of the electric floodlights fell across our faces from the
open end of the tent. In five minutes we were dressed and
standing in formation—Smith, number two-forty, on my right;
and Cowlcy, number two-forty-two, on my left.

But that was only roll call and calisthenics. They were
always the same. One could get through thcm without fully
awakening, and in the stockade we did not measure our days
by the clock or by the sun but by the bad things that happened, for in each day there were one or two that were different, if you were attentive and saw them.

At calisthenics everything was dark, except for the zone
where the hard light from the guard towers came down inside
the gates where we stood. The outer camp was invisible. All
you saw was the glint of barbed wire, if a spotlight moved, or
the ground at your feet. Nothing more. The light blinded you.
Besides, you didn't want to look at the faces of other prisoners.
It was not until the first moment of apprehension and uncertainty that we looked up and admitted that a new day had
begun, and that was always when we were ordered into line
to receive our breakfast.

The loudspeaker barked, and we moved forward with a

*13*

shuffling of feet and a clanking of tin cups. No other sound.

On that morning, as on all others, we ate in the predawn darkness under the electric lights, for we had been sentenced to hard labor from sunrise to sunset. At Quai Dong we did just that; nothing less, and nothing more. Thus we were required to use some of our sleeping time for morning and evening meals. Only at midday were we allowed to eat by the light of the sun.

That morning the mess truck was late, and so by the time we got our food we all felt a little better. The sky was turning gray. Visible objects were growing out of the distance: the hills, the beaches, the Quonset huts, and, farther on, the jungles. The guards looked more human when they were no longer silhouetted against the floodlights. You hated them less when they had faces.

Sometimes the food was warm; more often it was cold. But it was brought into the stockade from the main camp in big kettles without lids, and so it was no one's fault. Still, none of us knew from one day to the next which it would be, and the anxiety was communicated down the line of waiting men. Even if it was hot in the kettles you could not be sure of eating it before it went cold in the tin cups. That was worst in winter. Now it was August, when even the nights were no longer cold, so sometimes the food was warm.

It was coarse cereal, without milk or sugar, and black coffee. We had learned to eat it without complaining. They did not persecute us at Quai Dong; but there was a war going on, and, after all, they could not be expected to spend too much time on us.

Next we got our work assignments. That was at five-thirty, and it was the second moment of suspense of the day. But this was deliberate, for we were not allowed to know from one day to the next what assignments would be made, nor whom they would favor. Each day the work was carefully changed. This uncertainty contributed to the futility of our lives, and thus it was a regularized part of camp discipline.

The staff sergeant read the work details over the loud-speaker, standing above us in one of the guard towers. We paid no attention until he came to within ten of our numbers, for work parties did not go out in groups larger than ten. The camp was short of guards, and they did not like to bring men down from the main barracks just to watch us.

Cowley had once argued that we should strike for a work schedule, "So a guy could know what was in store for him from one day to the next." He spent one full night arguing, but he did not understand that not knowing was part of our punishment. Anyway, there was no way for us to strike. So we listened to the loudspeaker.

"Two-thirty-five to two-forty-five! Shovel sand! Pick up sacks and shovels! Report to main gate! Fall out!"

We did as we were told. Other details were already leaving the stockade and heading up the shore with hammers to crush gravel for the main camp. Some were going in the opposite direction toward the sand dunes, with field packs full of the same gravel, to fulfill their hours of penal marching. We considered ourselves fortunate; only Smith was worried now that we would not get a decent job tomorrow.

I had lost my ability to worry about tomorrow. One could never tell. We were given a guard and signed out by the sentry at the opening in the barbed wire fence. The guard led us through the free ground of the rest camp, past the huts where the Regular Army still lived. Soon we were outside the main gate, facing an orange sun that was rising through horizontal bars of fog on the seaward horizon. He stopped us at a likely-looking spot a hundred yards above the shore and told us to drop our sacks and go to work.

"You've got all day for it," he said, "but you can knock off if your barrow gets to the water before dark."

Then he lit a cigarette and walked slowly back up to the gate. There was no reason to guard us, for at Quai Dong escape was impossible. In front of us there was a long bay of shallow water that came in over the shoals from the South China Sea. At low tide a man could walk into it for a mile without getting out of his depth; but the tide came in with a rush, and he would drown. At our backs was the compound, surrounded by barbed wire—first the military stockade, with its guard towers and low tents arranged in narrow lines so that the machine guns could cover them in one burst; then the sprawling flat checkerboard of Quonset huts and fuel tanks of the main camp. Northward there was the peninsula and the sand dunes, and in the south and west nothing but the foothills and the jungles. They looked five miles away, but they were more than ten. It was too far. Now and then a man would try it, thinking, in his desperation, that he would live to reach Cambodia. Even if he made it over the hills he found only Army patrols, which would arrest him, or communist villagers, who would kill him. You could not survive in a land where you were the enemy. There was no escape, unless you could get to Japan. But that was impossible.

Now and then Army patrols went out from Quai Dong to bring back the bodies of prisoners who had tried to get away. Sometimes the local villagers told them where they had seen them lying. No one asked how they had died. From the point of view of Quai Dong it didn't matter whether it was dysentery, a villager, or an Army patrol. Usually there was nothing to bring in. Still, the burial details did their best, since the Army had to have the I.D. tags.

That morning we had been doubly fortunate, for we all knew that the guard was not supposed to tell us how long we had to finish a job. Once we knew how much time we had we could work fast and then rest, or move slowly, without really working at all, and know that it made no difference. In this way we were able to choose for ourselves, and to become free, if only momentarily. The futility went out of the work then, of course, and it was the futility that was intended to provide the punishment to which we had been condemned.

Soon our work detail was arguing over what to do.

"I say we oughta work fast and get it over with," Smith said, and the others agreed.

But Cowley, who had been there longer than any of us, shook his head and said that there was no point in it, because even if we built our sand mound to the regulation height all the way down to the water, we would have to go on working.

"They'll see us resting and put us to work somewhere else, before our time is up."

Cowley did not trust the guard. Perhaps he was right. Sometimes one guard tricked you, and then another came along and made you begin all over again, as if he did not know anything about it.

They couldn't decide among themselves, and finally the others turned away from Cowley and put the matter to me.

I told them that I didn't care.

Cowley had his way, and we set to work shoveling the

sand slowly into our canvas bags. Then we lifted them onto each other's shoulders and carried them the required sixty yards before allowing them to drop. The regulations said that the bags had to be full; otherwise they could force you to do it all over again, after dark, by spotlight, when everyone else was asleep.

In two hours we had scooped the sand out of a wide basin and transferred it to a low ridge which grew to resemble a burial mound, some twenty yards long. Each of us had carried about a ton's weight, but we were accustomed to it and had not worked hard. Only a new prisoner, who was nothing but a boy, seemed to feel it. He was shaking and white-faced, either because he was sick or because he was afraid, it was difficult to tell which. Smith tried to make it easier for him by telling him to half-fill his sack, but Cowley warned him to leave him alone.

"Let the kid do his job," he said, "or the screws will come down on him."

A Mexican, number two-thirty-six, grinned toothlessly each time he passed the boy with his sack on his shoulder. "He's scared of the work," he said, "because he don't know yet that it ain't the work that'll kill him at Quai Dong."

To me the only bad thing now was the sunlight. It was glaring up off the white sand. When I emptied my sack I walked back with my eyes closed to keep from going blind. Then, too, by eight o'clock one began to sweat from the heat.

"They'll make it worse for us tomorrow," Smith grumbled each time he dropped his sack on the mound.

At ten o'clock the guard stood up and came down to us and marched us back up to the gate, where we were given five minutes' rest. We were permitted to take one cup of water

apiece from the rusty barrel that sat just inside the gate.
Cowley sat down on the sand and carefully sipped his water
by himself, which was the proper way.

I dipped my cup and was slowly lifting it, so that I would
not spill a drop, when the Mexican said, "Look," and I turned
around.

"Up there," he said, pointing toward the dunes.

"It's a burial detail coming in," Smith answered.

It was then that I first saw the jeep, on the top of a sand
dune far up the peninsula, perhaps a mile away. At first it surprised me, for I had not expected to see any living thing on
that horizon.

"It's not a burial detail," Cowley said without looking up.
"Not from the north."

"He's right," another man said, "you've got to get west,
over the hills, to have a chance."

Cowley snorted. I wiped the sweat out of my eyes and
shaded them with my hand to see better. Whatever it was, it
did not seem to be moving. It was just sitting on the top of a
dune, jiggling up and down in the heat waves that rose off
the ground.

"What do you think it is?" Smith asked, moving close to
me and lowering his voice.

Cowley overheard and said that he didn't give a damn,
and I agreed, and told Smith to forget it.

Everything on that coast was a deception. It required no
effort of my imagination to convince myself that the jeep was
a fantasy, or a burial detail, or going in the opposite direction
from what it seemed, fleeing the compound. Even I, who had
no illusions left, had once seen a broad river flowing below the
treeless hills in the west, though I knew that there was noth-

ing beneath them but the steaming roof of jungle foliage. Things were never what they seemed at Quai Dong. Anything might happen there, but none of it would be of any importance; not, at least, for us. I had grasped that fact with difficulty, but now I held to it firmly, as a convict must. It alone made my existence bearable.

I sat down in the shade of the barrel and washed my mouth out with what water I had left and did not look at the jeep again. Once, when they had brought me to Quai Dong, handcuffed to the seat rail of a jeep, I had seen the compound from the sand dunes, rising and falling from view like a flat island on the horizon of a mountainous sea. Nothing seemed to move when you were in the dunes. They were all useless ups and downs. Yet, eventually, one got out of them—and then, after so much effort, there was only Quai Dong.

We were taken back to moving our sand. The guard marched us silently through the gate and beneath the wooden tower where the American flag hung like a dying leaf in the motionless air. We began to dig. The mound inched toward the shoreline, slowly, and slowly the cavity widened and deepened in spite of the sand that continually trickled back into it. By eleven o'clock it was filled with salt water that seeped up from below. We stumbled down the slope of the beach under the blazing heat of the full sun, with our heavy sacks breaking our shoulders, and we climbed back painfully one step at a time. The cup of water wasn't enough. Thirst returned almost as soon as we began to work. No one spoke now. We dug silently until, at eleven-thirty—the shadow of the guard tower nearest the gate had shortened just enough to touch the water barrel—a large company of convicts was marched past us to the water's edge, where they were ordered to go to work scraping the rust off the hull of the old landing ship that had been left on the beach when the camp had been built. It was the sort of work that the people in the headquarters liked best, since the rust would grow back within a week and could be scraped off again. The men were told to take off their shoes and roll up their trousers. Then they walked gingerly out into the water, as if the rocks cut their feet; but the water was cool.

"The lucky bastards," Smith said, and watched them for a moment.

But I looked at the LST, not at the men. The front ramp had fallen down and was buried under the sand. Now the waves eddied back against it, burying it still deeper. Dark streaks of orange rust drained from the portholes. The glass of the bridge was covered with thick salt spray. The thing rose over the shoreline, useless and entirely forgotten by the men who had come to occupy that coast. Its waterline was rusted through, and the sea made a sighing, patient sound as it ran in and out of its open bilges with the rise and fall of the tides. Soon, as the sea measured time, there would be nothing left of the steel hull, unless, perhaps, a ridge of rusting metal remained beneath the sand, roughly in the form of a ship's bow, upon which a man might cut his foot, if a man chanced to pass that way. The camp, and the Americans in it, would be gone much sooner. The thought filled me with indifference, and comforted me.

Even now the old wreck was destroying camp discipline. The work detail that had been sent to clean the rust from its sides was carousing in the water. We heard cries and splashes. For a moment the men were happy, and Smith watched them with a silent grin. Then some of the guards came down from the gate and put a stop to it. They hit one or two men with their swagger sticks, but it was only to keep up the form and everyone knew it. Then, too, one of the guards slipped in the water and fell on his back in the rocks. He limped back up to sit in the sun under the gate and dry out, and the prisoners went to work on the ship in a good humor.

Our life at Quai Dong was not without such moments of relief, which is to say that the system of punishment had not yet been perfected. Probably the staff was shorthanded and overworked.

The heat was getting worse. Everything was stoking up. We watched the cold salt water that leaked into the hole that we had dug, and our thirst grew harder to bear. We moved slower, and felt the effort of the work more. Then, suddenly, I realized that the sound of shovels digging in the sand and of hard breathing had stopped around me. I straightened myself painfully and saw that everyone, both at our work site and at the LST, was watching the jeep, which had finally made its way out of the sand dunes and was racing down the beach toward us. Now even the guards were on their feet.

This time Cowley asked me what it was.

I shrugged. "Nothing," I said.

"You guys get back to work!" the guard shouted when he heard our voices; and then, to divert us, he thought of a joke about jailbirds that can't fly, and he told it to us and laughed nervously.

But the jeep raced past us, throwing sand off its tires, and bounced up through the main gate. Two soldiers rode in the front seat, and another held on in the rear with a young Vietnamese sitting next to him with his hands tied behind his back. He wore the customary black pajamas. Then all that I could see was his back and his thin neck. When the jeep turned the fast corner at the gate the boy almost fell out, but the soldier next to him grabbed his collar and jerked him back. I glanced at Smith and saw a look of hatred on his face, though I had no idea whether it was for the young Vietnamese or the soldiers in the jeep.

"A prisoner, for Christ's sake," he said, and went back to his shoveling.

The guard asked us not to make it hard for him, and everybody started to work again; but I looked up and saw the jeep drive through the center of the camp, past the windowless huts, and stop in a cloud of dust in front of the command post, where the major's flag hung lifelessly from its staff. Then the three soldiers jumped out and dragged the boy up the steps after them. From that distance they again looked very small, like toys.

The guard was mad, and he poked me hard in the ribs with his stick. I started to dig in the hole again and forgot about the jeep. You didn't get a guard down on you, not if you had been at Quai Dong long enough to know how to survive. I had been there a year, and I had seen what could happen. There was nothing to be gained by resistance now, and a great deal to be avoided.

"The dirty pig," Cowley whispered. "I saw him stick you."

I told him to forget it, or he would get us all into trouble.

When the sun was directly overhead we got thirty minutes off for lunch. Ten minutes of it was for eating, and twenty minutes was for standing in line. But it was the expected thing, and we had learned to bolt our food. No one spoke, though three hundred of us were crowded in together under the silent machine guns of the towers. There was only the hurried sound of spoons scraping out the last bits of food from tin cups and the hard, watchful eyes of guards. It was strange to me that they only seemed to fear us when we were gathered together for meals, though it was the moment when we were the least likely to attack them, since we had barely enough time to eat. But then a stir passed through the mass of prisoners. It hovered over us like a whisper, and I heard a distant rumbling, a ripple of little dull concussions. I hated the sound of it, but it made my heart begin to pound so hard that I stopped eating and listened, in spite of myself.

An undernourished little man at my elbow opened his mouth, which was full of food, and said that it was heavy artillery. Several voices nearby agreed. A general discussion began.

"Eight-inchers," another man said, nodding his head and cocking it to one side to hear better. "Fifteen, twenty miles from here," he added. "Those are the big ones."

With that he grinned all around, though whether it was because he knew the sound of howitzers, or because he was safely out of their long reach at Quai Dong, I could not tell.

We had wasted time. The loudspeaker ordered us to re-form our lines, and I had to throw out part of my food. Cups had to be scraped clean for inspection. I swore at my luck, and we fell in on the sunbaked parade ground with a clanking of tin cups and metal shovels. Then it was perfectly silent.

Five minutes passed. Inspection was over yet no one moved, and we were given no work orders for the afternoon. We stood in the heat for thirty minutes longer, and still nothing happened, and no one spoke. Flies buzzed around my face. Sweat ran into my eyes and down my back. Here and there a man became restless, and one of the guards pulled him up hard with his swagger stick. All that I could hear was the crunching of guards' boots back and forth behind us, and the sound of distant guns.

Then the loudspeaker barked "Left face!" and when we turned I could see that at the head of each long line there was a slow shuffling of feet, moving toward the infirmary a half step at a time. We were in for shots, I supposed, though I could not remember if it was yellow fever or cholera. It hardly seemed to matter. But of course the Army had to inoculate us, like everybody else. The only difference was that we had to stand in the sun for hours without moving or speaking, and without being told what was going to happen to us or when we would be allowed to go back to work. But that was part of our punishment.

I let some of my weight rest on my shovel handle, very carefully, so that no guard would notice, and waited. Next time, I thought, if I had the chance I would steal an extra cup of water; though, since it was seldom possible, I would likely get caught. Then I would be in for penal marching in the sand dunes. But now I was sorry that I had not tried, for the sun was blazing directly down on our necks. There was a ringing in my head. I could see the little white blisters rising on the ears of the man in front of me. I watched them, fascinated; and then I realized that it was Smith, and that I had not known who he was. It worried me, and I wondered if I was getting sunstroke. I had seen what happened. They did not allow anyone to pick you up or cover your face until the line began to move and they had to step over your body. That was to keep us from malingering. Now and then men died.

I tried to hold in my energy, and I listened. Still I could hear that ringing sound. It was not in my head now, but it was growing nearer. Something unreasonable was going to happen—I could feel it, spreading from the jungles until it passed over us and reached out to sea. It was the madness.

I had seen it, once, and though I had forgotten it during my year of fighting, it had often been in my mind since I had come to Quai Dong. On a cloudless, sunlit day I had watched a gray cruiser sneak stealthily in against an empty beach. It was entirely alone. Then, for no apparent reason, it opened fire with all its batteries at a range of low inland hills. The guns went off furiously, each time with a flash, and then a muted thud, a dull *boom;* little compressions of air following one another across the miles of open water to where I stood, *boom, boom, boom,* and after each flash and thud a piece of the distant hills rose into the air and fell slowly back.

At first I had thought that I would see the hillsides covered with Vietnamese; but when I focused my binoculars I saw that the hills were as empty as the beaches. All that I could make out was a grove of splintered trees that sat in a low saddle between two peaks. Perhaps that was what the Navy was trying so hard to hit, though the trees had already been destroyed, and it seemed a waste to do it again. A very flat sound, *boom,* over the silent expanse of the South China Sea. I remembered that I had laughed to myself then, for the behavior of the cruiser had seemed absurd. Probably, however, I had been more frightened than amused, for I had been looking out of a porthole on the troopship that was taking me to disembark at Saigon, from which I was expected to lead thirty-five men into battle.

But now I was no longer afraid. All that was behind me. I closed my eyes and listened—I could hear that they were still shooting, somewhere, far away, and it filled me with indifference. The sound itself was harmless, only a thump against the ear. It might have been distant thunder or sheet lightning, but I glanced cautiously at the sky and saw that there was not a single cloud. Then the sound rolled over our heads again, at once somnolent and formidable: unmistakably artillery, but very far off, on the other side of the hills, firing northward at something that was still further away. At a peasant's hut. At a tree. At nothing. The silly bastards. I stole a glance at the flat line of the seaward horizon. There were no illusions there. It looked like burnished copper, hard and empty.

Finally my turn came. I reached the door of the infirmary and they told me to leave my shovel with the guard outside and take off my shirt. The walls of the room were dirty, but it seemed more or less cool after the sun's heat.

Dr. Mason looked up. "Hello, Kreuger," he said. "How do you feel?"

I told him that I was all right and looked away. Finley and two other medics were giving shots at tables that had been set up in front of the other doors. Behind each of them stood an M.P. with his .45 open in his holster.

Mason tapped a file that lay open on his table, and told me that I was in for typhoid. "You'll be a little sick from it," he warned. "Don't worry."

"No," I replied.

He gave me the shot, and then he listened to my chest. "Cough," he said.

Then he went around behind me and thumped my back. "Drop your trousers and bend over."

I did it, and watched the wall in front of me. When he was finished he told me to pull up my trousers and wrote something in my file. Then he closed it and looked up at me.

27

"Take this with you," he said, and shoved a thin newspaper, neatly folded, into my trouser pocket. He put it in deep, without the guard seeing, for we were forbidden, of course, to have anything to read at Quai Dong. I told him that I didn't want it, but he said that it was the Copley *News* and that I might change my mind. I thanked him, since there was nothing else to do.

"Did you hear the artillery?" he asked, lowering his voice and pretending to be busy with a vial and a needle.

I nodded. "Yes," I said, "I heard it."

"That's the first time we've had it that close to Quai Dong. What do you make of it?"

"Nothing."

He glanced up at me, then he lowered his eyes and said, "They're killing some fresh heroes. They never remember how bad the old ones smelled."

I didn't say anything. Mason was a fool to talk like that to a prisoner. Even an M.O. had to be careful at Quai Dong.

But Mason didn't seem to understand. He waited silently, as if he were testing me. I didn't like it because I didn't see what he thought he could gain by it, or how he thought he could help me. Still, Mason was the only one of them that I didn't hate. He alone, of all the men at Quai Dong, seemed to realize that something corrupting was happening to us—not just to the men in the stockade, but to all of us. Once I had seen him sitting alone under the lee of the LST, as though he could stand the camp and the major's company no longer and had gone there for solitude. He had risen slowly to his feet when he had seen me watching him, and he had looked at me with suspicion. Now he looked at me with friendship, as if we understood one another. Probably, I thought, it was just that he was fed up with it and wanted to get out. But Mason knew that I had been an officer. No doubt he had heard of my trial, and he took his meals with the major in the officers' mess; therefore I did not trust him.

When I refused to answer he nodded approvingly and taped a wad of alcohol-soaked cotton over the needle mark on my arm. Then he squeezed it with his fingers and held it tightly for a moment.

"How long were you in the Army, Kreuger?" he asked.

"Three years," I answered, wanting only to get away from him.

"Did you learn anything?" he asked with a humorless smile.

I looked at him for a moment. "I learned to keep my head down," I said.

"Remember that," he replied, "and you'll be all right." Then he gave me an impersonal nod of his head and told me that I could go.

I retrieved my shirt and shovel at the door, puzzled and irritated by Mason. For a moment I was blinded by the daylight outside, but I found my way to the familiar sweat-stained backs of Cowley and Smith, who were standing motionlessly in the rear of the line of men that faced away from the infirmary, waiting until the last had received their shots.

"Now do you see what would have happened if we'd worked to finish our barrow and knock off, like the screw said?" Cowley whispered. "We'd be standing here, with everybody else, just the way we are!"

I could feel the thin newspaper in my pocket. I wanted to throw it away, but I couldn't do it without being spotted by a guard. Anyway, it might get Mason into trouble—though it was likely to get me into trouble if I kept it. You didn't have anything to do with anyone if you wanted to survive at Quai Dong. I knew that the typhoid serum wouldn't hit me until the middle of the night, when I would be able to sleep it off. I would only be a little feverish and have strange dreams. Sometimes I didn't mind it too much. It was a little like getting drunk.

It is possible that I began to doze. Whatever happened, I found myself being shouted at by a guard who stood ten feet from me. His face was red and screwed into a grimace.

"Kreuger!" he hollered; and then, with his hands ominously gripping both ends of his swagger stick, he shouted, "Number two-forty-one!"

I pulled myself to attention, and he told me to fall out and come with him. By the angle of the sun I judged it to be two o'clock; therefore I had been standing for one hour without a thought crossing my mind. I recall thinking that death could not be much different.

Cowley was taken out of the line too, and we were marched together to the gate and handed over to a Negro soldier—not a guard, but an ordinary soldier from the rest camp. He signed for us on the day sheet, and then he and the guard saluted. I watched them, thinking that it was strange that they should salute one another.

The soldier was young and frightened. Perhaps he had been warned that we were dangerous. No doubt we looked tough, dressed in our stockade uniform, sweating from our work, with our faces streaked with dirt. He gripped his carbine across his chest with both hands and ordered us to march

ahead of him up to the command post. It annoyed me to have
to obey him, but he was too scared for me to be able to risk
asking him why we should go there, and so I did as I was told.
Once I glanced back, for no reason, and looked at the line of
waiting men who remained inside the stockade fences. There
was Smith, standing with two conspicuously empty places behind him—and I saw Dr. Mason standing in the doorway of
his infirmary, watching us being taken away. He raised his
hand as if to encourage us, then let it fall. The soldier told us
to step lively, in his boy's voice, and I turned around. We
walked in silence through the main camp, past the rows of
dusty huts, and across the dirt parade ground, where the heat
waves rippled like water.

When we reached the headquarters a staff sergeant with
a neatly trimmed moustache and a starched uniform came out
on the porch and asked me if I was Kreuger. I told him that
I was, and he said, "Come this way, please." He was very
polite and had obviously been given special instructions.

The four of us walked around to the maintenance yard.
Rows of trucks were drawn up behind another barbed wire
fence, their windows blinded by dust. Drums of gasoline
stood nearby, too hot to touch. We passed an empty jeep, and
stopped in front of a windowless shed. The sergeant told us to
wait outside, then he went in through a low doorway. After
a moment he opened the door and told us to go in.

At first I couldn't see anything inside the room. It seemed
as black as night, though there was a small electric light burning in the ceiling. Slowly, as my eyes grew accustomed to the
gloom, I made out three figures standing beside a heavy table.
One of them had lieutenant's bars on his collar, and a cigarette
in his mouth. I could see its glowing tip better than I could

his face. The other two stood a little behind him. The Vietnamese boy was standing against the opposite wall with his head down, bent forward from the pressure on his wrists, which were still tied behind his back.

The lieutenant took the cigarette out of his mouth, and said, "Which one is Kreuger?"

"This one," the staff sergeant answered, pointing to me.

The lieutenant studied me for a moment, then glanced at Cowley.

"What the hell is that?" he asked.

The sergeant didn't seem to know. There was a moment of complete silence. Finally Cowley himself moved forward cautiously and said, "Private Cowley, sir, number two-forty-two."

"I don't give a damn who you are," the lieutenant snapped. "I want to know what you're doing here." He glared suspiciously at Cowley, who only looked back without opening his mouth again, as if he knew nothing about it.

"I asked only for Kreuger," the lieutenant said, turning to the staff sergeant. "What the devil went wrong?"

The staff didn't know. He looked at me, then back at the lieutenant. "The guard that brought them up from the stockade must have made a mistake," he said.

The Negro was called in and questioned, but he didn't know anything about Cowley either. The lieutenant began to swear, which seemed to worry Cowley.

"They called me out of the line," he insisted doggedly.

"No sir, not me," the Negro protested. "I only took hold of 'em at the gate. It was the guards inside the stockade that brought 'em out to me. I didn't tell him nothin'."

The lieutenant turned his back to us and looked at the light bulb. "Then how in hell did he get in here?"

The Negro was silent. Cowley moved quietly toward the door, eager to get away, but the lieutenant stopped him. "Oh no you don't!" he shouted, and faced Cowley with a deadly look, as if he were worried only at the thought of Cowley getting out and had forgotten that he had not wanted him at all. "You're in this with the rest of us now, and you're going to stick it out until we're finished, like it or not."

The staff sergeant straightened himself up and said that he could keep him under wraps in the headquarters, if the lieutenant wanted him to.

"Don't be an ass," he said, and told the sergeant to post a sentry outside the shed and to keep him there, away from any contact with the rest of the camp. "Now get out of here," he said, and the staff sergeant left.

Cowley moved uneasily back against the wall, as far out of the way as he could get; but the lieutenant seemed to feel easier once the door was locked. He forgot Cowley and turned around under the dim light and put his cigarette back between his lips.

"This is Sergeant McGruder and Sergeant Nguyen, our ARVN interpreter," he said, introducing me to the two other men who stood at the table. They nodded slightly to me and looked at my prison clothing. "I'm Lieutenant Buckley," he added. "Do you still remember your Vietnamese?"

I told him that I did. "A little," I said.

"Good," he replied, turning toward the boy and dropping his cigarette, which he crushed under his feet. "We're going to conduct a short interrogation."

Cowley began to swear under his breath. I moved as far away from him as I could without approaching the center of the room, where the table stood. The prisoner was staring at its metal surface. He hadn't moved since we entered the room. I watched him while the man called McGruder and the man called Nguyen wired up a second and brighter light from the ceiling. Then I understood what was wrong, for the boy's face was suddenly illuminated by the hard glare of the powerful bulb that they switched on. He raised his head and looked directly into the light, as if he wanted to blind himself; and I saw that his chin and mouth were covered with blood.

"The interrogation shouldn't be very difficult," Lieutenant Buckley said.

CHAPTER *TWO*

I WAS WELL TRAINED, after so long a time at Quai Dong, and I looked carefully around the room for the safest place, if anything should happen.

There were the six of us and the prisoner in a room that was thirty feet long and half as wide, and the table took up a quarter of the space. It was made out of heavy sheet metal and had strong vises at either end, as if it had once been a workbench. Above it was a low ceiling of corrugated tin, sagging in the middle where the rusted sheets had been bolted together. All the heat in the room seemed to come down from that ceiling. It leaked in under the sagging plates like lava. The walls, too, were made of tin sheets. The ruts of the corrugated surface did not look comfortable, but I had a prisoner's instinct to keep my back against something, and I marked the hot corners of the room as a retreat. On the wall opposite the door there was a tool rack that stood as high as a man's head. It was divided into thick plywood boxes, black with grease, and each box was marked with a number that had been burned into the wood. The tools had been thrown in on top of each other by the last occupants of the room, but I could see the gleaming black handles of wrenches and metal hammers. Deeper back, where the electric light did not reach, there were dark coils of rope and wire cable. The floor was dirt, hard-packed from use, and as dry as the parade ground. Only the cots were new. For the moment they gave the room

**37**

an odor of new wood and canvas that almost covered the musty smell of tin and human sweat.

Then there were the faces: Cowley's heavy, ugly face, squinting up at the light; and McGruder, as ugly as Cowley, but with no humor around his eyes or mouth, watching the prisoner; and Buckley's handsome pink face, clean-shaven, with his pale blue eyes moving from place to place; and finally Nguyen, whose impassive, patient eyes were fixed on Buckley. Only the prisoner seemed to want to see nothing. He kept his face lowered out of the light and fixed his eyes on a long streak of rust that ran down a leg from the top of the table, as if the metal were slowly bleeding.

Suddenly I wanted to get out, but I had been carefully taught that escape was impossible. I tried not to think about it. The soldier, Russell, was still holding his carbine at the ready. He looked frightened and dangerous, as if he might squeeze the trigger and shoot through the ceiling.

Not that he wanted to hurt anyone. For the time being, I didn't think that any of them wanted that. They only seemed frightened or unaccountably angry.

Buckley and Nguyen began to argue quietly between themselves about how to begin with the boy. Buckley was in a hurry, but Nguyen was telling him that "such things" took time. Finally Buckley turned his back to the light and looked at us. "You all know why you're here," he said, "and what we have to do."

"Let's get it started," McGruder said.

"No, we're going to do it properly," Buckley replied sternly, and McGruder moved away with a shrug and watched the crack of sunlight under the door.

"Now listen to me," Buckley said, raising his voice, though we had heard him perfectly well before; "we're a rest camp and a military stockade. We don't have the right people to do this kind of job, but we're going to do the best we can and get it over with. Now," he added, stepping forward and dropping his voice, "I've got a Vietnamese interpreter who says this thing will take a long time. Do any of you think you can do better than that?"

"Let me have him, Lieutenant," McGruder said, and he turned toward the boy hopefully—but Buckley was looking only at me and seemed not to hear.

"Kreuger?" he asked.

"I don't know what you want," I said.

Cowley dug his fingers into the back of my arm. "Keep out of it!" he whispered.

I wanted to tell Buckley that I did not know why I was there at all, but Cowley was right; it was safer to be quiet and I said nothing. Among the six of us in the room nothing seemed clear. I did not know if Cowley and I were counted with the interrogators or as convicts. We still wore our prison uniforms. Our position was awkward, and if something went wrong it could be dangerous, for we would be witnesses to whatever took place. Buckley knew it as well as I did, but he tried to hide it from us.

"You're here as an officer," he said.

"What about Cowley?" I asked.

Buckley shifted his feet and did not answer for a moment, then he frowned up at the light. "We've had trouble from a local guerrilla outfit for a month. We need your help. Forget the stockade."

"I thought the district was pacified."

"It is officially pacified," he said, tightening his lips, "and we want it to stay that way."

"What does the boy have to do with it?" I asked, despite the pressure of Cowley's fingers on my arm. Finally I felt his hand slide down, and he let me go.

McGruder turned around slowly and looked at me. "We took him off the Weichu Road," he said. "He was trying to get through our patrols."

I watched McGruder for a moment. He looked at me full of hate, as if he thought that I was somehow a threat to him or to what he wanted to do. I wanted only to stay clear, but there was no way to tell him that.

"What will happen to the boy?" I asked Buckley.

"Leave that to us," he replied quickly. "You do your job and you'll come out all right."

I agreed with him, since there was nothing else for me to do, and I retreated to one of the cots along the walls and sat down where I would be able to watch what happened from the farthest possible distance. Cowley followed me. All that puzzled me was what my "job" was supposed to be. It was not until I looked up across the room at Buckley that I realized that I had turned my back to an officer and walked away. I had taken a seat, in spite of my prison khaki, and had not been immediately jabbed with a swagger stick and ordered to get back on my feet. That had never happened to me before at Quai Dong. Only then did I realize how much of our punishment in the stockade had been made up of simple humiliation. Already, somehow, I had acquired this simple privilege. I was grateful to Buckley. I couldn't help it, and that made me distrust him.

Still, it seemed that we had been granted a reprieve for as long as the interrogation lasted. At the moment that was all that mattered. I thought of Smith still working on the beach, trudging from the hollow to the shore with his sack full of sand. Or maybe they had not yet been released from the stockade yard. Then he was still standing bareheaded in the heat of the sun. No doubt he wondered what had happened to us. Probably he thought that we had been taken for special punishment and was glad that he had been left behind. For a moment the thought amused me. The room was even hotter than the beach, for there was no air in it, but it was out of the direct rays of the sun. The corrugated shed would be a diversion, at the very worst. All that remained was to make the most of it and to keep out of the way of whatever was about to happen.

Cowley, however, put another face on our good luck. He leaned close to me and asked me if I knew why they had brought me to the hut instead of taking someone from the regular camp.

"I know some Vietnamese," I said, watching the prisoner's head.

"They've got a translator," he whispered. "What the hell do they need you for?"

I shrugged. "We'll find out soon enough."

"Use your head," he said. "Guys in the rest camp go back to the States after a year out here. They can talk and make trouble. We're easy to keep quiet because we aren't going anywhere."

He added that he had seen interrogations before; and then he grinned ruefully, as if to make the best of a bad thing.

I began to ask him what he meant, though I understood

**41**

it well enough, when Lieutenant Buckley suddenly turned
impatiently away from Nguyen, with whom he had again
been arguing about the prisoner, and rapped the table angrily
with his knuckles to silence us.

"This is no joke," he said, raising his voice again, but now
to an official tone, as if he were about to address a staff meeting. "We need definite information about these guerrillas, and
we need it fast. We've finally got a prisoner of war that can
tell us everything we need to know, and our Vietnamese ally
says that he'll need at least a day to make him talk."

McGruder said, in a very matter-of-fact way, that the
guerrillas might attack again somewhere during the night.

"You don't need to tell me that," Buckley replied.

He was so earnest that he couldn't stand still. Yet it was
what he said, not the way he moved, that made me uneasy,
for certainly McGruder and Nguyen knew perfectly well what
they had come to do. Therefore Buckley was speaking only
to me, which was either dangerous or foolish, depending on
what he meant by it.

"They've hit us everywhere," he said. "Fuel dumps, quar-
termaster convoys, rest camps. Last week they mined the
road to Doc Thieu. At dawn we lost a jeep and three men."

He added that all the attacks had come at night. It seemed
to be a personal affront to him. "In six weeks they've cost us
fifty casualties, and as far as we know we haven't killed one
of them yet—or if we have, they carry their dead with them.
This is a little peasant outfit. Saigon says there isn't a hard-
core Viet Cong in the district. All the help they're getting from
the outside is equipment, and they're careful with that. They
don't take on combat units. Only isolated patrols or a single

vehicle. They like to win," he added, "and so far they've had it all their way."

He looked angrily at the boy—the prisoner—and said that he was one of the guerrillas. He called them Victor Charlies, as was the custom at staff briefings. I glanced up at the broken tin roof, thinking more about the heat than what Buckley was saying. He turned around and looked down at me as if to gauge the effect of his words. Of course none of it meant anything to me, and I didn't try to hide it. Buckley frowned with disapproval and nodded to McGruder.

"Show the lieutenant what the prisoner was carrying," he said. He used the title that was no longer mine, as if to place me still further in his debt. I began to hate Buckley a little.

McGruder swung a string of grenades off his shoulder and held them up to the light. "They were rolled inside the little bastard's blanket," he said, and, for the first time, he seemed satisfied that things were going the way they should.

I recognized the grenades, as they doubtless knew that I would. They were Chinese, in a North Vietnamese Army sling. I felt a dim memory of anger, of ambushes and night patrols, but I did not let McGruder see it.

"It's clear that he was running supplies for the guerrillas," Buckley continued, as though he were satisfied with his evidence. "The patrol that took him off the road found drugs on him as well as grenades. Now all we have to do is make him tell us where he was meeting his contact, and our job is finished." He cast one last official look around the room. For a second he even looked at Russell, but Russell only gripped his carbine tighter and stared back at him.

"Saigon says that this zone is a military backwater," Buck-

ley said quietly, watching the boy's lowered head. "A rest
and recreation camp and a stockade. The entire district stinks
of it. According to the brass, we have nothing to do out here
but sit on our ass and play cards. We're a joke in Saigon bars.
I've heard it. Well now," he added, "we've got a little opera-
tion of our own, a tough little guerrilla outfit that just asks
to be cut up—and we're going to do the job without any outside help, no interpreters from division, no Special Forces
people butting in where they don't belong. This kid is our
first break," he concluded, looking at each of us in turn. "He
can lead us to their base and supplies, and by God we're going
to make him do just that."

Cowley and I sat perfectly still. We had nothing to say.
It seemed simple enough, to hear Buckley tell it, though it
**was** their job and not ours. I wondered why they had sent for
us at all, since they already had an interpreter who knew more
Vietnamese than I did. There seemed nothing for me to do,
and even less for Cowley, who was good for nothing but
fighting.

However, Buckley told McGruder to untie the prisoner
without offering us any further explanation, and the boy was
brought under the light. The interrogation got under way.

Nguyen began the questioning slowly. Buckley was almost
immediately moving back and forth from one wall to the
next as if he could not control himself now that his ignorance
of the language had forced him to surrender the proceedings
to Nguyen. He seemed to consider the business an urgent
affair that had to be finished in the shortest possible time.
Within the hour, if Nguyen could do it; before sundown, at
the latest. Buckley chain-smoked, but the cigarettes didn't
help him and he kept pacing around the room. Now and then

he glanced down at me, as if I had somehow let him down; but he said nothing.

We waited. There were no provisions for the night in the room—only the heavy table, the bare light bulb, and the three cots without blankets. Not even drinking water had been brought in. The walls were bare except for the tool crib, but the tools were no part of the interrogation, as far as I could see. We seemed to be locked in alone with the prisoner.

Nguyen asked him where he had gotten the grenades. When I listened to the Vietnamese, which only Nguyen and the prisoner and I could understand, I felt even more alone than I had before. Buckley, McGruder, and even Cowley could not follow me as far as my understanding of the language forced me to go. I didn't like it, for it made me feel a party to anything that Nguyen said, but there was no escaping the sound of his voice in that small room.

I looked up to see what the boy's answer would be—and it was then, for the second time, that I felt the uneasy certainty that something unreasonable was going to happen. It was happening. I could not connect the frail-looking boy with Buckley's account of guerrilla raids and dead Americans. I knew better, but I could not do it. And yet Buckley, and McGruder, and even the quiet Nguyen looked at the prisoner as if he were unquestionably the enemy, and were all waiting only to hear his confession, not to hear the truth, whatever it was.

When I looked up at the boy's face, caught under the cruel light, I saw only the stiff black hair, the delicate forehead, the high cheekbones, the small brown eyes that hardly moved behind their tightly drawn lids, the full, impassive mouth, and the narrow chin where the blood had dried and turned

**45**

black—and stamped on it all was a look of immovable fear, as though he were staring at death, without hope. I knew that face. It bore sisters and daughters who were beautiful—for the face was inherently feminine—and who now filled the brothels in Saigon. And I had seen it, and a hundred of its brothers, in the quick glimpses of highland skirmishes; and once, the last time, I had not been able to see the enemy. Only the face itself. Disembodied. Waiting. I was kneeling in tall grass at the mouth of a valley near Darlac when it happened to me. Barren hills rose on three sides of us. Our captain had been killed in the morning, and I was left in command of two hundred men. Four other companies of infantry were dug in on the ridges on top of the hills, ready to open fire on the remnants of a Viet Cong outfit that we had trapped on the floor of the valley. My job was simple. When the company commander on the hilltops had his machine guns and mortars in position—the anvil—I was to give the order for my men to move in. We were the hammer: machine guns, grenades, flame throwers, automatic rifles, and finally bayonets. There would be no survivors, unless we took one or two prisoners out of the valley for questioning. The Montagnard tribesmen who would move through the valley after we had gone would see to that. I watched the Vietnamese trying to dig in, sweeping my field glasses from one knot of them to another; and then, perhaps because the sun was hot on my back, or because I was tired, I began to see, not the enemy, but faces. Only faces. Here and there I would glimpse them for a fleeting second, unreal through my glasses, enlarged, yet tense, expectant, certain of death. Suddenly two mortar shells exploded among them, taking the range. My radioman signaled me. I took the receiver and heard the order to attack when the barrage lifted.

My company was braced, waiting. I waited too, kneeling in
the sunlight, listening to the whirring of insects in the tall
grass, gazing at the small figures of the men we were about to
kill—and then I pulled my company back. The men were
veterans and they obeyed my order. We opened up one end
of the valley like a hinged door and withdrew up the side of
the hill to our left. The Vietnamese were quick and they fled
through the gap before the outfits on the hills understood
what had happened. There were one or two mortar hits. A
few men were killed. But that was all.

At my court-martial I was accused of refusing to obey an
order under fire, and of "aiding and abetting the enemies of
the United States." I was given legal counsel, an Army law-
yer from the Military Justice Division. He pleaded that I had
suffered a nervous breakdown; "combat fatigue," he called
it, and cited my past record to show that I had been a good
soldier and, as he put it, a patriot. He was a hard-working
man and I bore him no ill-will. The court found me guilty of
willfully failing to obey an order under fire, which was only
right, and was about to sentence me when a colonel dropped
in—I don't remember his name—and discovered that I knew
two thousand words of Vietnamese. He asked me if that was
true, and I said that it was. Then he decided that I was Army
property, and too valuable to be disposed of entirely; and
thus it was that they only broke me to the ranks and sentenced
me to hard labor in the camp at Quai Dong, where my two
thousand words would be available if anyone wanted to use
them.

Once or twice during the first weeks of my imprisonment
I was called to the major's quarters to interpret. A village
headman complained that his chickens had been stolen; the

mother of a dead child wanted compensation for its funeral. Then they seemed to forget about me, and my days went on undisturbed. No doubt someone mislaid my file; or, which seemed more reasonable to me, they had decided that I was unreliable and could not be trusted.

Now I was expected, once again, to look at a boy's face and see the face of my enemy. It was very remote from my life after so long a time at Quai Dong, where there were no enemies and no friends, but only endless days of waiting. Still, Buckley and the others showed no doubt. Obviously, I was expected to follow their lead and to make my stand with them. We were to show solidarity in the face of the enemy. Yet it seemed a difficult question, and it was one, moreover, on which the Army could no longer force me to give an answer.

The other questions that Nguyen asked the boy, the simple ones that centered around concrete facts like hand grenades and medicines, were always the same; the boy's answers, too, were identical each time. It puzzled me at first, then it became tiring to hear. But Nguyen seemed undisturbed by it, as if he had expected it. The prisoner's replies were made in a voice so low that it was barely audible. That, too, was irritating to hear, for, though I did not want to listen to any part of it, I could not keep from straining to catch his words. Only later did I realize that it was difficult for him to speak through his broken lips.

"Where did you get the grenades?" Nguyen asked. He spoke with a razor's edge to his voice, though his voice remained quiet. Unlike Buckley, he did not have to shout.

"From the dead soldier," the boy replied humbly.

"Was he American?"

"North Vietnamese."

"Where was he?"

"On the road to Weichu."

"There are no dead soldiers there."

"He was in a ditch."

"Why did you take the grenades?"

"To protect myself."

"Where did you get the medicine?"

"From the dead soldier."

"Soldiers of the Democratic Republic of North Vietnam do not carry penicillin and morphine!"

"This one did, sir."

"Where were you taking your supplies?"

"I was going to Saigon, to my sister."

"The Weichu Road does not go to Saigon."

"There was fighting on the other side of the hills. I was afraid to go that way."

"You will tell me now," Nguyen said, "where you were told to meet your comrades."

"I am alone, sir. I was only going to my sister. Our parents are dead."

Nguyen studied the boy's lowered head for a moment, then he turned to Buckley. "You see," he said, "he is obstinate."

McGruder approached with a businesslike expression on his face, but Buckley waved him back before he could reach the table. He told Nguyen to begin again. "Keep after him," he said.

Nguyen put the same list of questions to the boy. Buckley began to pace back and forth between the close walls of the room. I watched him, for I was already tired of watching Nguyen. It seemed reasonable enough, I thought, for him to want to find out where the guerrillas were meeting to launch their raids. He was impatient and angry, but he looked honest. I supposed that if he broke the prisoner's resistance he would be able to save some lives and do his career some credit. There was little enough chance for that at Quai Dong.

But when I looked back from Buckley to the boy, who had been dragged off the Weichu Road and locked in a window-less room with four Americans and a Vietnamese that he could not trust, it all seemed more questionable, somehow, than when I looked at Buckley alone.

"There's no way of knowing whether he's a guerrilla or not," I observed quietly.

"What do you mean by that?" Buckley snapped, looking at me for the first time as if I were a convict.

Cowley nudged me hard, and I said nothing more.

But McGruder was aroused. He looked at me vengefully, as if he had been waiting for me to make a mistake, and said that you could never tell one Vietnamese from another until he shot you. "But we caught this little son of a bitch red-handed, and we ain't gonna let him off!"

I admitted that he was right, but still he wasn't satisfied, and told Buckley that Nguyen was wasting time. "Throw the Chinaman out of here, Lieutenant," he begged. "Let's do it our way."

I saw the boy's arms stiffen when McGruder raised his voice; and I knew then how his mouth had been covered with blood.

McGruder saw his involuntary motion too, and a look of pleasure came into his eyes. "I can make him squeal like a monkey," he said, and took up a threatening position behind the boy, not quite touching him but so close that he must have felt his breath. McGruder's head nearly touched the hot bulb, but he was too interested in the boy to feel anything. For a moment I hated him. I was fascinated and sickened by the thought of driving my fist into his unshaven jaw. But I stopped myself, for I did not want to get involved, and I leaned cautiously back and listened to the droning sound of Nguyen's voice, which went on undisturbed in spite of McGruder.

By three o'clock the interrogation had made no visible progress. I passed the time watching a cockroach moving in the shadows along the floor. It was pushing its snout against the wall behind Cowley's foot, trying to find its way out. The floor was dirt, but the metal walls had been driven in too deep for it to have a chance. Still the bug felt up and down, inching along. But it was going in the opposite direction from the door, where it must have come in. There seemed no reason to step on it. If it was patient and went all the way around, behind the heels of the other men in the room, it might find its way out; if not, it was its own fault.

From time to time I listened to the questioning. It remained unchanged, and the prisoner's answers remained identical. Finally I saw that Nguyen was forcing the boy to repeat his meaningless replies by quietly menacing him if he varied them in the slightest way from the answers that he had first given. The word-for-word repetition puzzled me. It was wearing on everyone's nerves. But I supposed that there was a ritual that they would observe before the boy would tell us anything, since they were both Vietnamese in the presence of Americans, however much they might hate one another.

Certainly, after the first hour, the boy looked tired. Probably he had not slept for a long time. If he had been trying to get to Saigon he had most likely been walking for days. Of course, if he were a Quai Dong guerrilla, it didn't matter; but I began to number the uses that a peasant might have for hand grenades, and especially for medicine, without being a Viet Cong. I could imagine several—the black market in Saigon for one—but it was none of my business, and I kept quiet. It didn't seem to be Nguyen's business either, for he had not asked the prisoner about it. He simply went down his original set of questions, as methodically as if he were performing a mass.

Buckley, however, was not taking it with Nguyen's equanimity. He dropped one half-smoked cigarette after another, ground them angrily under his heel, and told Nguyen to hurry up.

"We're wasting time!" he complained.

McGruder grunted and looked at the back of the boy's head. "He's afraid to hurt him," he said.

Nguyen denied it—he seemed to fear that accusation above all others—but he was silenced by a wave of Buckley's hand and told to continue in whatever way he thought was best.

"Only be quick," Buckley repeated. "We don't know when the guerrillas will attack again."

Buckley looked down at me and added that every minute that we lost might cost an American his life. I said nothing, and Nguyen turned back to the prisoner and began over again from the beginning, but he warned Buckley to be patient.

"He is very strong," he said, gazing at the boy's lowered face.

McGruder began to swear under his breath.

"I do not mean physical strength," Nguyen said, looking at McGruder with contempt and speaking in his slow but strangely fluent English, the tone of which seemed to aggravate McGruder even more than what Nguyen said. "I mean a stubborn spirit, which is much stronger. That is why you must not injure him again. Pain will not break his spirit. It will only kill his body. We must exhaust him, then he will be willing to betray his comrades."

"If I hit him," McGruder muttered, "he'll talk."

"No, he will only die, and thus escape us."

McGruder turned red and made a motion toward the fragile-looking Nguyen, but Buckley told him to keep away. Then he turned to Nguyen and asked him how much longer it would take.

"Two, maybe three days," Nguyen answered, studying the boy's face intently.

"But you said it would only be a day and a night!" Buckley shouted.

"I did not know then how strong he was," Nguyen said, straightening up and facing him.

Buckley ran his fingers through his hair and moved away from the light. "We can't wait that long," he said, shaking his head and shoving his hands into his hip pockets. "The major will never stand for it."

Again McGruder asked to be put in Nguyen's place. Buckley ignored him, lit another cigarette, and sat down. And then, without warning, he turned to me.

"What do you think?" he asked.

I shook my head, and told him that it was none of my business.

"I'm only asking your opinion."

"I don't have one," I replied, suddenly hating Buckley for trying to draw me into his game again, whatever it was going to be. Now I understood what Dr. Mason had wanted to tell me. Mason was an officer. He must have known what the major and Buckley wanted to get out of the boy. He had tried to warn me, and I was sorry that I hadn't listened.

But it was too late for that now. Silence was my only defense. I refused to say anything more. Buckley glanced up at the boy's head, then he looked back at me and shrugged, as if to say that he had done his part and given me my chance and that now anything that happened to the boy would be my fault, not his.

"Do what you can, Nguyen," he said, and settled back against the wall.

McGruder moved quietly away from the light, apparently satisfied from the tone of Buckley's voice that his time would come, and Nguyen began his interrupted questions from the beginning. Now I understood more of his method, and I feared the room in a way that I had not before. Nguyen was not angry at anything that the boy might say—the answers themselves became meaningless when they had been repeated a hundred times. Even the words lost their accustomed sense and were reduced to nonsense syllables, like a chant in an alien tongue. Nguyen asked him, for the hundredth time and with no change whatever in the expression of his voice, where he had found the dead soldier. And the boy answered, for the hundredth time, "On the road to Weichu."

"There are no dead soldiers there."

"He was in a ditch."

"Why did you take the grenades?"

"To protect myself."

"Where did you get the medicine?"

"From the dead soldier."

"Soldiers of the Democratic Republic of North Vietnam do not carry penicillin and morphine!"

"This one did."

Nguyen stopped. Slowly his hand came up, and the boy said, "This one did, *sir*."

"Where were you taking your supplies?"

"I was going to Saigon, to my sister."

"The Weichu Road does not go to Saigon."

"There was fighting on the other side of the hills. I was afraid to go that way."

"You will tell me now where you were instructed to meet your comrades!"

"I am alone, sir. I was only going to my sister."

Then Nguyen, without allowing a second's rest to mark the completion of the cycle of questions, asked again where he had gotten the grenades. The boy answered as he had always answered, and the rhythm of the questions was repeated. It was maddening to listen to, and I tried to ignore it, for I saw now that Nguyen's purpose was not intelligence, but simple exhaustion. He would wear the boy down until he was too weak to give any answer at all. Then, I supposed, he would have a way of extracting whatever he wanted from him. They would beat the boy's mind into a shapeless mass, and in it, like splinters of broken glass, they would find what they had been looking for. But the end was a long way off, and it was obvious that someone would have to relieve Nguyen from time to time. The strain was more than one man could bear— and with a sudden halt in my thoughts I realized why I had been taken from the stockade into that room, for I, who had escaped a military prison because I spoke two thousand words of Vietnamese, was Nguyen's replacement.

I got up instantly and crossed the room. "Am I supposed to interrogate him?" I asked Buckley.

He looked up at me and seemed pleased, as if he had known that I would come to ask him that question, sooner or later. "Not entirely," he answered, and moved over to offer me a place to sit down next to him.

"I won't question the boy," I said. I warned him that I'd go back to the stockade first. The hut looked less like a reprieve than it had at the beginning. I didn't know if they could do anything more than send me back to the stockade, but I was ready to risk it.

To my surprise Buckley gave me a friendly look and told me to sit down. When I did, he lowered his voice and spoke under the steady droning of Nguyen's questions.

"Can you understand what they're saying to each other?" he asked.

I listened for moment. "Yes," I said reluctantly, "I can."

Buckley was pleased with me then. "Good. All I want you to do for the present is listen to what they say. Don't let a word slip by, not one word." He squinted up into the light and said, "We'd be fools to trust Nguyen."

"They're only repeating the same thing," I said. "It's meaningless."

"I don't care. We'll let him do it his way for now; but they're both Vietnamese and they'll try to stick together."

"I doubt it," I murmured, yet there was no way for me to know whether Nguyen was in earnest with his interrogation or not, since I had never seen an interrogation before and had no idea how one was carried on. I glanced at Buckley. Now I understood still more of what Mason had tried to warn me to stay clear of. Something had changed in the room. It had somehow become smaller. It seemed to give me less room in which to hide. Gradually I realized that the cost of my simple act of crossing from one wall to the other had been the loss of my immunity. I had wanted only to defend myself, and to warn Buckley that I would not interrogate the boy, but something had gone wrong. Perhaps, if I did what Buckley wanted, I would gain a degree of power. But I did not want the power. I wanted only to stay clear. Cowley was scowling at me from across the room, and Buckley was smiling, as if he understood perfectly what was in my mind and had been counting on it. Now he thought that I was his man.

"If Nguyen doesn't break him soon," he said, "we'll have to do it by ourselves."

Buckley watched the two figures who stood under the light, but he was leaning so close to me that our shoulders touched. Some treacherous idea was fixed in his mind. That much was clear to me, and I drew away from him. But it was not clear to me how I was supposed to convince him that he was wrong. The only way for me to stay clear now was to stop the interrogation, but I had no way of doing it. Perhaps Buckley was right and Nguyen was protecting the boy. It meant nothing to me in either case, and that, at any other time, should have been enough to keep me out of it—but it was not difficult to see that if Buckley lost confidence in Nguyen entirely he would be left with no one to carry on the interrogation but myself, unless he gave the boy to McGruder. I glanced at Buckley's face. His eyes were fixed on the boy, waiting, and it was then that I realized that it was he, and not

I, who had gained a degree of power. I was deep in the trap with him now, with no way out.

But of course there was no need for apprehension. Thus far everything was under control.

Another hour passed. The voices of Nguyen and the boy went on with the deadly regularity of a ticking clock. McGruder sat on the cot along the back wall, apparently passive, with his head covered by his hands and only his knuckles visible. Nguyen stood in front of the table with his back to us, his round shoulders and his short-cropped head in the light, and went on with his even and methodical questioning as though he were conscious of no threat to his position. The walls of the tin hut creaked in the heat. The boy's voice was a weak whisper, into which Nguyen jabbed each question before he could recover his breath from the last answer. The boy was allowed no rest, and he seemed to be losing ground. The torture was mental, a slow dulling of the senses. I found myself becoming fascinated by it; then, looking up, I saw that Russell was no longer in the room.

"He's outside," Buckley said, "standing guard duty."

"Why?" I asked, getting off the cot.

Buckley looked at me and shrugged. "We have a prisoner," he said.

"There's a fence around the motor pool, and there's barbed wire around the entire compound. Nobody's going to get away."

"It's normal security. Why does it bother you so much?" Then he added, with a grin, "You should be used to barbed wire by now."

I walked to the door, but I did not open it, nor could I look out. There were no windows in the hut, not even an air vent through which I might have seen the sky, or the stars, if it was already night. We were entirely sealed in. The heat was suddenly unbearable. I wanted badly to see what was outside, for in that closed place I seemed unable to trust my memory of what I had left behind. I thought of the beach, and of Smith; but they were both far away, beyond reach. I hated the thought of sentries outside the door, though I had never felt it so strongly before. But then I saw that Buckley was watching me with too much interest, and I moved away from the door.

Suddenly I heard Cowley shout, "Look out!" Instantly there was a loud crash behind me and a wild cry of anger.

When I turned around I saw the prisoner lying on his back in the dirt six feet from the table. McGruder, who had knocked his cot over to get at him, was standing alone under the light, panting, as if he couldn't breathe.

"He'll talk now, by God," he whispered.

Nguyen had been thrown aside, but he was already accusing McGruder at the top of his lungs. "You are a fool, Sergeant McGruder!" he yelled, losing his self-control. "You are a barbarian!"

"You're chicken-livered," McGruder grunted. "I swear to God I'll kill him if you don't get it over with."

"And do you think you can make him talk then?" Nguyen shouted.

McGruder turned slowly away from the boy and Nguyen backed out of his reach. Buckley stood up. For the first time since the interrogation began he looked calm and untroubled. He quietly told McGruder to get out of the hut. "If you attack the prisoner again," he said, "I'll have you put in detention."

To my surprise McGruder turned his back and went out-side without a word. There was a flash of sunlight when he opened the door, and I saw that it was not yet night.

"Kreuger," Buckley said, without looking at me, "see if the prisoner is all right."

I should not have moved, but I had been conditioned too thoroughly in the stockade not to obey—at least once—and I went past Cowley, who had jumped to his feet when McGruder hit the boy and was standing in a corner, ready to fight his way out of the room if he had to. When I bent over the boy I saw that his eyes were open, but dazed.

Nguyen leaned over my shoulder. His face was inexpres-sive again, as if nothing had happened. He reached down and took the boy by the chin and turned his head sharply from side to side. A thick swelling was rising on his left temple, but it was not bleeding.

"He is all right," Nguyen said quietly, and helped me pull him to his feet. The boy weighed less than a girl, and I pulled too hard and nearly upset him. Nguyen took him away from me and dragged him back under the light, but when he re-leased him his knees buckled and he collapsed on the floor. We picked him up again, but he couldn't stand by himself. Nguyen finally left him sitting in the dirt with his head lean-ing to one side, and looked up at Buckley. "You see that we cannot go on," he said bitterly.

"Stand him up," Buckley ordered.

"It is no use if he cannot speak," Nguyen answered.

Buckley turned around. "All right," he said, and rubbed his hand across his mouth, "bring a medic."

I didn't look at anyone in the room. Not even the boy. My

only instinct was to keep my head down, no matter what happened.

Finally it was Cowley who spoke up. "They're all down in the stockade giving shots."

"Get one up here then," Buckley answered impatiently.

Cowley hesitated. "It's outside the gate," he said.

"Damn it, I don't care where it is! I gave you an order! Do you know who you're talking to? I want a medic in here, and I want him fast!"

Cowley left without another word, and Buckley controlled himself. The three of us remained in silence, staring at the prisoner's face, waiting for a sign of life. Somehow I did not expect Cowley to come back—if I had gone I would not have come back—but finally he did. I suppose that he could think of no way of getting out either. He brought Finley with him. Cowley remained next to the door and Finley looked around the room, still blinded by the sun's light, as if he saw none of us.

"Revive him," Buckley said, pointing to the boy who still sat in the dirt with his back slumped against one of the heavy legs of the table.

Finley glanced at me, but when he received no sign of recognition he knelt beside the prisoner and began to examine his mouth and jaw, where he could see the dried blood.

That irritated Buckley. "It's his forehead that's hurt," he snapped.

Finley saw his error then, and he left the boy's mouth alone and cleaned and bandaged his temple. Then he gave him a shot of something that looked like water, but which made his head begin to roll from side to side.

"All right," Buckley said, "can he stand up?"

"Yes sir, I guess so," Finley answered, stepping back cautiously, as though the floor were mined.

Again the boy was pulled to his feet. This time he kept his balance, although his eyes were open abnormally wide and his breathing was shallow and hard. Then the drug seemed to wear off and his head fell into its lowered position once more. All that I could see was the pressure bandage on his temple and his eyes, which were blinking rapidly, as if he were dizzy or afraid. He looked smaller, as if something had broken inside of him, but he stayed on his feet.

"Get back to work," Buckley ordered, and returned to his cot, where he picked up the cigarette that he had carefully laid aside when McGruder had knocked the boy down. "You may find the prisoner more willing to talk now," he added, and leaned back against the wall to watch.

Buckley looked satisfied, as though things had finally taken a turn for the better. Nguyen didn't say a word to any of us. He simply began his interrupted questions again. The only difference was that now there was a new sense of urgency in his voice, as if he too felt that his time was running out.

At first the boy did not answer, for the rhythm of the interrogation had been broken. McGruder's fist had allowed him to rest. Only when Nguyen's voice fell across his face like a whiplash, again and again, without mercy, did his broken lips open and begin to form the ritual phrases once more. He spoke now as if he were in a trance, but after a few moments his answers and Nguyen's questions slowly fell back into their accustomed pattern.

The sound of it was worse now than before, when it had

looked as if it would go on undisturbed for days. Now we could see that it was only an interlude, and that at the end of it the boy would be hurt again. Yet the combined sound of their voices was almost worse than the sight of the boy's damaged head lying face-down in the dirt. McGruder's attack had freed us from the sounds of the interrogation, if only for a moment. Now the deadening murmur of it filled the room again—and I wondered, with a dropping in the pit of my stomach, how many times the prisoner could recover and go on.

Finley moved noiselessly around the room, keeping his back near the wall and staying out of the circle of light where Nguyen worked the boy. He sat down next to me on my cot, where I had taken refuge when the interrogation got under way again. Soon Cowley joined us, and the three of us sat together. Cowley was very quiet now, and seemed to be waiting only to see what direction things would go. Finley glanced about the room nervously. "What's this all about?" he whispered.

"Nothing," I said; then I added, "Guerrillas—they think the kid was on his way to meet the guerrillas with supplies. Nguyen's trying to find out where."

"Oh," Finley answered, as if it made sense to him, and then he stared up at the boy and at the ugly string of grenades that McGruder had left on the table under the light. "Is he really a guerrilla?"

I shrugged. "Most likely."

Finley said that he had never seen a guerrilla before. He studied the fragile neck and shoulders of the boy; then, for no apparent reason, he turned to me and asked if Dr. Mason knew about it.

I was sick of Finley. His innocence was worse than McGruder's sadism. Not even Mason could help us now. "I suppose the doctor knows as much as any of us," I said, and then I stood up and moved deliberately toward the door.

All that I wanted now was to get out. Nothing else mattered. I saw that Cowley had been right; they had used us because we were convicts and they thought we had no choice. But they were wrong. We had nothing more to fear and, being outsiders, nothing whatever to gain from the interrogation. They did not understand that only men who still had something to hope for could be made to do such things. They could send me back to the stockade, under the harmless muzzle of Russell's carbine, as they had brought me to the room. Cowley and the medic could take care of themselves.

I was past Nguyen and the boy, who faced each other under the hard light, chanting their litany of question and answer as if they could keep it up for weeks. Then I was beyond Buckley, who made no move to stop me, and I held the door knob. To my relief it turned in my hand. I stepped out into the heat and the blinding sunlight without looking back, and turned away toward the jeep and the open gate.

And then I saw the barbed wire. Russell and three new guards were pulling it up throat-high around all sides of the hut. Now there was a third ring of barbed wire, and we were alone inside of it. In the sunlight it looked black, like a barren hedge of thorns, but metal, impassable. Only a six-foot zone of free ground remained between it and the tin walls. McGruder was there, sitting to my right with his back against the shed, regarding his heavy boots, waiting with doglike tenacity. Outside the fence I saw Russell watching me. Four carbines were stacked within his reach, with fixed bayonets, ready; and far away, through the coils of the second fence at the motor pool, were the distant tents of the stockade and the guard towers, shimmering patiently in the heat—and far beyond them, down the flat slope of the white beach, outside the main gate, I saw the old wreck and beneath it the tiny figures of men splashing in the water under a green sky, as if they were free.

CHAPTER *THREE*

"O F  C O U R S E you can leave, Kreuger," Buckley said, and stopped his pacing to look down at me. "But let me warn you, as a friend, that you'll do penal march for the rest of your time at Quai Dong. Have you seen the sand dunes?"

Buckley smiled. It was night. Five more hours of the relentless sound of Nguyen's voice had gone by, and the end was not yet in sight. I had finally asked Buckley to release me and let me go back to the stockade. Now he was standing in the middle of the room, moving impatiently about with his hands on his hips while Finley revived the boy, who had again collapsed. He looked angry, but he was pleased, nevertheless, to have heard me ask a favor of him. No doubt it made him feel better to see that if he could not manipulate the prisoner as he wanted, he could at least control the rest of us.

"Then we're in detention here," I said, feeling too tired to move. I had seen the sand dunes. They were a place where a man could do nothing but die.

"Call it anything you like," Buckley replied, looking at me with his hands thrust into his pockets. "The fact remains that the major has ordered me to seal this room off. No one leaves unless he's under special orders, and no one enters who isn't prepared to sit it out with us. We've got a prisoner, Lieutenant, and the word isn't getting out—not through anyone."

Cowley frowned ominously. He shuffled his feet behind me

like a schoolboy wanting to defend himself before a head-master, but unable to find his words. I wanted to protest, too, for we had been forced to come. We had been given no choice. But I watched the boy's eyes slowly open, and did not answer. It was futile. We had no rights. We were there only to be used.

The prisoner was sitting on the ground with his back and head resting against a leg of the table, naked to the waist. His face was sunken with fatigue. He looked as if he could not stand anymore, but again Finley's injection had been too strong for him to fight against. When he lifted his face to the light he seemed to remember where he was. He closed his eyes and pressed them shut. Buckley saw that he was conscious and he stopped his pacing. He faced the boy and told us to get him on his feet.

"He's faking," he said. "Stand him up."

This time I ignored the order, but Finley, who did not yet understand what was happening in the room, raised the boy and forced him to stand. He was dizzy from the sudden jerk upward, and he began to sway from side to side as if he would faint again. Then Nguyen, whose methods were becoming more desperate as the hours of the night wore on, stepped forward and jabbed his groin with a small blade that he hid in his closed fingers. It hardly drew blood, but the sharp stick of it was enough to force the boy to jerk upright and to resist his own fatigue, and thus to cooperate with his interrogators. Finley drew back, horrified at the knife, and stared at Nguyen.

"You're torturing him," he whispered.

"Only when it is necessary," Nguyen said.

Cowley reached out and took Finley protectingly by the arm and drew him back against the wall, out of the light.

"We must keep his attention from wandering and finding

relief," Nguyen said, looking strangely after Finley. "He is beginning to weaken. It is for his own good."

The prisoner had been standing on his feet for more than eight hours now, with the hard light falling directly across his eyes. He had not been allowed to shift his position to ease the pain in his legs. He stood less erectly than he had in the beginning, but he had not given in and I had thought that he had won. Then Nguyen drew his little knife, and I understood at last that there was no hope of the boy's winning.

When Nguyen stuck him with it the second time I left the hut, my face burning. I was too angry to stay in the room any longer, though it was none of my business what they did. Outside there was nothing but darkness, and in the distance one or two blurred lights. The night was thick, as if a fog lay on all sides of us. Not even Russell and the other sentries were visible, though I knew that if I reached my hand out I would touch the barbed wire. Somehow it was impossible for me to remain standing alone in that dark place, imagining what lay just beyond. I tried not to move, but I found that my anger was gone when I faced that empty blackness; and I went back inside the hut, where Nguyen had the boy standing stiffly under the light with a look of pain on his face.

I recorded the fact with apprehension—that the prisoner's face would show pain. I had hoped that he would be impenetrable, as an Oriental should be. Only McGruder, who had been allowed to come back to the room at dusk, seemed unaffected by the new method. He watched without apparent emotion. Finley was quiet—Cowley had seen to that—but he was pale and withdrawn now that he understood what he faced. Buckley had grown more tense and excited than ever, and even Nguyen was more earnest in his work than he had been at the start, as though the interrogation, which was still made up of nothing but the endlessly turning cycle of identical questions and answers, had entered a new stage with the collapse of the boy's attention and the introduction of the knife. The smallest reaction of his face had become of great importance to Nguyen. And now the boy, who had fainted in spite of the knife, was once again standing on his feet with his veins pumped full of the drug that Finley had forced into him.

The interrogation went on. It was clear now that it would go around the clock. Cowley had been sent outside to carry in the food that was brought from the mess and laid just inside the barbed wire, as one feeds animals. Not even the guards were allowed to bring it into the room. The empty cans were stacked by the door, waiting for Cowley to take them out and put them back where he had found them, so that they could be taken away. We had drinking water, and blankets, and we had all eaten—with the exception of the boy, who had been forced to stand and repeat his answers alone while Nguyen bolted what food he could. We were prepared for the night.

The interrogation went on without change, and without any apparent hope. Again and again Nguyen asked the boy where he had found the grenades, and again and again he answered, "From a dead soldier."

"Was he American?"

"North Vietnamese."

"Where was he?"

"On the road to Weichu."

"There are no dead soldiers there."

"He was in a ditch."

"Why did you take the grenades?"

"To protect myself."

"Where did you get the medicine?"

"From the dead soldier."

"Soldiers of the Democratic Republic of North Vietnam do not carry penicillin and morphine!"

"This one did, sir."

"Where were you taking the supplies?"

"I was going to Saigon, to my sister."

"The Weichu Road does not go to Saigon."

"There was fighting on the other side of the hills. I was afraid to go that way."

It went on without end, and at the turn of each cycle of questions Nguyen demanded confession. "Tell me now where you were told to meet your comrades!"

And always the boy said, "I am alone, sir. I was going only to my sister."

The only variation came when the prisoner tried to change an answer, or was unable to repeat it, or forgot it entirely, as if his mind had begun to rebel at the words and would not hold them any longer. Then Nguyen used the tip of the knife. But such diversions were rare. Mostly it was repetition without error, and therefore without interest. I wondered how long Nguyen could hold out. He was tough, but the strain of the questioning was greater for him than for the boy, for he had to keep pressing the interrogation forward, while the boy had only to answer in the prescribed manner, which seemed relatively easy since the answers were always the same. By now the boy could recite them in his sleep. All of us could. The knife, I supposed, had been introduced to prevent just that. Still, it was obvious that sooner or later Nguyen would have to rest, and I tried to steel myself against the pressure that I knew they would put on me to take his place. Now that the little knife had become an accepted part of the interrogation, I was more determined than ever to keep out of it.

Not that I was afraid to hurt a man. It was easy with a machine gun at two hundred meters—I had done that. Maybe, if I were left with no other choice, I would do it again. But it was just such a choice that I did not want to make in that room, for it was not so easy to stick a boy with even a quarter of an inch of a knife when you were forced to look directly into his face as you did it. If he had remained impassive it might have been possible. The unmoved face of an intended victim would infuriate any man. I knew that, and I did not believe myself to be any different. But the prisoner did not cooperate. He showed pain when Nguyen used the knife, and that made it unbearable to see.

And he used it often. As the night hours passed the boy's strength waned and his answers became more and more irregular. Buckley listened closely, his face expectant, thinking that the prisoner was about to confess. He was angry and tired, but it was clear that he had not given up any more than the boy had.

"You're taking too long," he warned Nguyen from time to time. "We've been in here more than ten hours. How long will it be?"

Nguyen went on with the regularity of a machine, and said nothing. Yet each time that Buckley spoke Nguyen pressed the questions, and the knife, with more force. When he saw that, Buckley seemed reassured. Then he smoked quietly for a few minutes before he began to pace again. Usually he made the circuit of the walls once for every four cycles of the interrogation that Nguyen and the prisoner completed. At times, however, the boy's replies stopped altogether, as if he could

not go on. Then the room was filled with silence, and Buckley
threw his cigarette away eagerly, certain that he would not
need another, and rushed to the table—only to hear the boy
begin again. At other times the boy's lips moved but the words
were unintelligible, or, worse, they were not those that our
ears had grown accustomed to hearing.

"What's he saying?" Buckley demanded, edging closer,
thinking that he had won at a cheap price.

"Nothing of importance," Nguyen answered, unwilling to
stop the interrogation for even a minute. "He is only talking
about Saigon. His mind is wandering."

Buckley stood over the boy to hear better, though he could
not understand a word. Then he glanced at me, his eyes burning from sleeplessness and distrust. It was when Nguyen saw
that look in Buckley's eyes that he used the knife ruthlessly to
return the boy's answers to their customary form, and to satisfy
Buckley. Thus Buckley gained more power. He soon learned
to use it, and Nguyen had no choice but to press the point of
the knife against the prisoner's thin groin until the halting
sentences were forced out of his mouth. Then he continued to
work it inward until the answers were rapid and exactly the
same as those with which the boy had first answered hours
before, so that Buckley would leave the two of them in peace.
Sometimes a red mark would be left on the boy's flesh. At first
I thought they were only little hemorrhages under the skin—
bruises. But, now and then, if the boy was too slow in his replies, the withdrawn blade would be followed by a few drops
of blood, which ran down an inch or two before they dried.
Within an hour the boy's groin was covered with these little
wounds. I was amazed to see that Nguyen never looked down
at them. I tried not to.

It was the face that interested Nguyen, not the groin. It was in the eyes and around the tight muscles of the mouth that he read the effect of his knife, and, what was of more interest to him, the slow effect of his voice; for it became clear that it was with his voice, not with the knife, that he intended to break the prisoner's resistance. It was a question of pride, perhaps, or of skill. Whatever his motive, he made the deliberate and relentless futility of the repeated questions his cruelest weapon. Only the boy felt the knife. All of us felt the corrosive power of Nguyen's voice, and we were forced to share the prisoner's agony, like the guards who stood with us in the stockade yard in the midday sun.

Nguyen's method was simple, and he had stopped once to explain it to us when Buckley's nerves had snapped momentarily and he had angrily demanded to know the reason for the seemingly useless line of questioning, which he had made me translate for him and which he knew went nowhere.

"I gained much experience in Saigon before the war," Nguyen said, turning to Buckley with a look of dignity. "I myself studied for a time in the university. Later, most of our prisoners were students. I have dealt with many this boy's age. It is only necessary to outlast them and they will beg you to permit them to confess. They are very strong-willed, but they lack endurance. They cannot hold out, if one is careful and prevents their escaping through death."

What they had taught Nguyen in Saigon was a system of interrogation that made the victim the cause of his own torment. The interrogator began with a set of questions—any questions—to which the prisoner gave answers that were taken to be false. Then, instead of going on to other questions, to which the prisoner might invent other false answers, the interrogator returned to the original set and went endlessly down the list, as Nguyen had done, requiring the prisoner to make exactly the same answers that he had first made. At the beginning the prisoner was puzzled; then he realized that he was trapped, caught in a cycle of his own false answers, or, if not false, of meaningless answers that were repeated over and over until the mind wore out. What seemed like a joke at first became futile irritation within a few hours. Within a day it was maddening torture. All that was required was time, sufficient patience, and the impossibility of escape.

"His resistance will be broken much sooner by this method than if we change the questions and try to trap him," Nguyen said, addressing Buckley as if he were speaking to a child, "for then he would be able to use his imagination and remain alert. This way his mind will become numb. If we are patient he will collapse, and then he will answer any question that you put to him, as if he remembers nothing else."

Buckley was skeptical. "You don't give him a chance to confess," he said.

"Ah, I do," Nguyen said, his dark eyes glowing, "but you do not listen!"

Nguyen was right. I had heard him change the cycle of questions from time to time to offer the boy the chance to rest, without feeling the knife, by confession. Thus far the boy had not yielded. Still, Nguyen assured us that such infrequent offerings of escape would become an irresistible temptation as time wore on.

"Now he thinks only of his comrades," Nguyen said, watching the boy's face intently, "but soon he will begin to think only of sleep and of silence."

When Nguyen had last given him a chance to confess, the boy had collapsed as if the sudden and unexpected release from the hypnotic strain of the never-ending, never-changing cycle of questions had drained him of all his remaining strength. Now he was on his feet, full of stimulants. The knife was once again in judicious use. The process was continuing.

"Each time that he refuses to confess," Nguyen had said, "I start from the beginning. He will not know how long it will be before I will give him another chance to escape by giving up his information. It is very hard to bear. In time he will come to blame himself. He will see that everything is his fault, and that we are his benefactors. Then he will accuse himself to us, and it will be over."

Buckley was restless at the thought of such a slow process, but he approved of the idea that everything was the boy's fault. I, too, could perfectly understand Nguyen's method, for it was founded on hopelessness. The prisoner was not forced to roll a stone uphill nor carry bags of sand. But his torment was worse, for, by being made to repeat his first ill-chosen words in an endless cycle, he was deprived of his very thoughts, which alone made it possible for a man to go on without giving in to his persecutors. That was simple punishment. Nguyen's method was intended to destroy, not merely to punish. I glanced at McGruder and knew what his way with the boy would have been. Direct, no doubt. Nguyen's intention was cruel, but his method drew little blood and I could stand to see it. It was almost fascinating, for he was killing a mind, while the rest of us had never killed more than a man's body, and that in combat, at more or less long range, as if by accident.

But the deadening sound of Nguyen's voice was destroying more than the prisoner. Once McGruder had leaped to his feet.

"I can't take any more monkey talk!" he shouted.

Nguyen went on as though he had heard nothing. McGruder looked around the room with a puzzled expression and had not made a sound since, as though he had gotten rid of all his hatred of Nguyen, and of the sound of the alien language, in that one wild shout.

Finley and Cowley showed the effects of the deliberate monotony of Nguyen's voice too. They were tense and nervous, and had receded as far from the center of the room as the walls would permit.

But the one who felt it most was Buckley. By nightfall the tin walls had contracted into a low-ceilinged box with three bare sides of corrugated metal, surrounding us with vertical bands of light and dark, like prison bars. The naked shadows stood motionless in the white glare of the electric bulb against the rack of ugly tools until the prisoner fell, or Buckley's nerves snapped and he began to pace back and forth, swearing under his breath—and then the shadows suddenly leaped into life, they twisted and elongated themselves and then shortened on the walls and the ceiling and the floor. It was a maddening dance that made all of us long for the softness of daylight; though we knew, now, that there could be no daylight in that sealed room. The only way to get away from it was to close your eyes; but you saw things in that darkness that were worse than even the metal table and the light.

Buckley had created the box, but he was wearing out in it. At times he sat on his cot with his head in his hands for so long that he seemed to be asleep. Then he would start up and look instantly at Nguyen as though certain that he had missed something of importance. After that he would look at me, and I would nod my head foolishly to assure him that I had been listening to the interrogation, and that Nguyen had not betrayed us—as if the words of the interrogation had any meaning in themselves. But he refused to be reassured, and stood up and began to pace impatiently from one wall to the other, around the table, behind Nguyen, until his movements became more irritating than the carefully grinding sound of Nguyen's voice.

Finley sat next to me, shaking his head. "When are we going to get out of here?" he whispered each time he saw Buckley on his feet.

It made me angry to hear him ask that, for it focused my certainty that we would be the last to get out. I ignored Finley, but I watched Buckley with a new desire for revenge. He was breaking up; I, at least, would survive.

Once he became so restless that he opened the door of the hut and looked out at the night, but when he did so I saw the surprised face of one of the sentries suddenly illuminated on the other side of the barbed wire fence. He was standing in the rectangle of light that the open door threw into the darkness, peering into the room, trying to see what we were doing that required such secrecy. He saw the prisoner, and Nguyen's knife.

Buckley slammed the door behind him and vanished. There were muffled voices. Someone cried out. When he came back the guard was no longer in sight, and Buckley did not open the door again. He remained in the room, as much a prisoner now as the rest of us, standing or sitting, never sleeping, and with no way to escape the killing sounds of the interrogation. He must have known the words of the Vietnamese by memory, though he could have formed no idea of what they meant. I knew now that they meant nothing except a slow form of torture.

I began to wonder then if a quick ending to the boy's resistance could be much worse, either for the boy or for those of us who would have to see it. I, too, succumbed to the peculiar strain of that eroding sound. Perhaps it was the lack of sleep, or the fear. Once I nearly stood up and swore at McGruder, for no good reason except that the muscles of my body demanded that I move or that I fight. As time passed my mind began to wander. I became deaf to the prisoner's voice, but not to Nguyen's; or to Nguyen's voice but not to the prisoner's. Then I heard only the whispered answers and thought that I would go mad, as if spiders had found their way beneath my clothing. I believe that Buckley once ordered me to stand behind Nguyen and listen with my ear next to his mouth; but that was absurd, and I must have dreamed it. At any rate, I didn't move.

Finley would not leave me alone. His fear was worse than my own. Probably he sat next to me because he knew that I was a convict, like Cowley, and could not order him to do anything in that room where to do anything was to incur guilt. Buckley had to shout at him to make him revive the prisoner when he fainted. Finley went to do his job with greater reluctance each time, and he returned to sit by me as quickly as he could. I saw that his hands began to tremble when he gave the injections, which alone permitted the interrogation to continue. Not that I blamed Finley. Like the rest of us, he had no choice.

"He'd be better off dead," he whispered to me, then closed his eyes.

He was developing the habit of rubbing his face. I didn't think he would last the night.

It is possible that I slept. Perhaps I only sat with my eyes open, and saw nothing. I revived sometime near midnight and found Buckley sitting next to me. Finley, who had remained by my side for protection, had been driven away. As if I could protect him. I was not sure that I could protect myself. But I tried to gather my thoughts together, for I could see that Buckley had come to the inevitable point of needing me. I had foreseen it, and I did not like it. A few hours before, I had been on my way to the sand dunes as far as he had been concerned, for then he had still expected a quick end to the boy's resistance. I had not been needed. That suited me. Now he sat next to me in the attitude of a fellow officer and listened with me to the sounds of an interrogation that promised to go on for days.

"Where are the questions now, Kreuger?" he asked, after waiting patiently, as if to give me time to wake up.

It was necessary for me to force myself to listen carefully. The sounds of the Vietnamese, repeated for so many hours, had lost all meaning for me.

"The boy is telling Nguyen that he was going to his sister in Saigon," I said.

Buckley nodded slowly and rubbed his face. "I didn't think Nguyen was making any progress."

"That depends on how you look at it," I said. "The boy has fainted twice, not counting the time McGruder knocked him down."

"I don't like this any more than you do," he answered. "Anyway, it's no harder for him than it is for us."

"We don't feel the knife."

"Listen to me," Buckley said impatiently, "I'll put a stop to this as soon as he tells me what I have to know! There isn't any other way out, not for him or for us."

"Maybe he told Nguyen everything that he has to tell," I said quietly, without looking at him.

"No," Buckley replied emphatically. "I won't believe it. The kid's lying. He wouldn't give an honest answer to us if his life depended on it."

Buckley was convinced that the boy was a Viet Cong, and I sat quietly and listened while he went on. I didn't care what he thought—since I knew nothing about it, one way or another—but it made me uneasy to see him able to speak about it with such certainty. It seemed to me that we should have kept our eyes on the ground and exchanged our words in whispers, like dwarfs. But Buckley did not share my scruples.

"There's only one thing we have any right to be interested in," he said, "and that's where this boy was to deliver his supplies. After all, what's happening is his fault. None of us wanted this."

My best defense was silence, and I said nothing further. But suddenly Buckley laid his hand on my shoulder, as if we were comrades-in-arms rather than jailor and convict, and began to expound his philosophy. He spoke in a very low voice. I listened, thinking not about what he was saying but that now he was under perfect control, while he had been on the edge of a breakdown an hour before. An idea—a fixation—had entered his head and restored him. He had come to a decision. Obviously, it included me. My only concern was to keep out of it.

"You know as well as I do that we have a moral duty to perform," he said, and he tried to describe it in detail. He seemed to enjoy saying the words out loud, as if once spoken in the hearing of another man they became irrefutable. Mostly what he said was that we had to sacrifice our good will toward "this boy," as he called him now, no matter how painful it might be for us to see.

"There's no other way out," he concluded, sweeping his open hand in front of him like a flat sword, decapitating opposition. "We'll have the blood of a hundred men on our hands if we don't see this thing through to a finish."

I neither answered nor moved beneath the weight of his hand.

That made him impatient again, as if my silence had contradicted him. "If you can tell me a way to both spare this boy and save our own men, I'll listen! But if you can't, you have no right to keep your hands clean while the rest of us do a dirty job that has to be done." He waited, and then he added, "You see, Kreuger, it's a simple question of loyalty. Nothing else."

He was toying with casuistry. I knew instinctively that it was contemptible, but I could offer no alternative—except to release the boy—and Buckley knew it. We had no choice if we were going to count the fate of the hundred men whose lives, he said, hung in the balance of our decision. We were the prisoners then of our own knowledge; but it was precisely the value of our knowledge that troubled me.

"You seem very eager to sacrifice yourself," I observed.

Buckley jerked his hand off my shoulder. "For Christ's sake, the kid is a communist!"

"I draw no conclusions."

"The guerrillas could be hitting us somewhere right now, while we sit here arguing! You don't have a right to do nothing when something like this has been dropped in your lap."

He went on for a moment, exciting himself by the sound of his own voice, about responsibility, and valor, and cowardice. No one else could do it for us, he said. Then he calmed himself and began again.

"Kreuger, you can't get away with this. You're going to have to choose. Either you're with the kid, or with us. There's no middle ground left."

He waited, thinking that now I would have to answer. But I wondered, instead, why he always said that it would be a hundred men. I supposed that it made it easier for him to have his way with the prisoner, since he thus made the moral odds a hundred to one in his favor, no matter what happened.

Still he waited, peering into my face, and for the first time I noticed that he was a remarkably handsome man. He had even tried to conciliate me by referring to the prisoner as a "boy," which he had steadfastly refused to do before. Thus he flattered me, and placed me in his debt. Good breeding demanded that I make an equal concession. Sitting that close to him he looked perfectly humane, and I reflected, in spite of my better judgment, that it was possible that his only motive was the desire to save American lives. Certainly I wanted to believe that it was, for then everything would be made easy for both of us—we could both have what we wanted most. For me it was simple freedom. I didn't care what it was for Buckley. But, by accident, I looked up at the prisoner. He stood on the other side of the table, and I saw his frail shoulders and the vertebrae in his thin neck illuminated in the light that hung over his drooping head. I did not look at Buckley again. The prisoner was real. The hundred men seemed suddenly very uncertain.

"I wouldn't go too far with the boy," I said.

"No," Buckley replied, "no further than we have to," but the tone of his voice was distant and absent-minded. I saw that he was watching Nguyen again and seemed to have forgotten about me.

"I don't trust him," he whispered passionately, clenching his fists and glaring upward at him so that I saw only the whites of his eyes.

Buckley filled me with disgust. I wanted him to go back across the room and leave me alone. Not even the sand dunes seemed intolerable anymore. "I want no part of this," I said. "I'll translate for you, but that's all."

Buckley seemed not to hear me. He continued to work his fists together, frowning up at Nguyen as if lost in thought. "It's only a game he's playing," he said. "He's trying to ruin the kid the way the Reds brainwashed our boys in Korea. All I want is information." He turned suddenly to look at me, and added vehemently, "So help me God, that's all I want! The kid can go to his sister in Saigon, for all I care, once he tells me what I have to know."

Somehow Buckley's final words unsettled me more than anything else that he had said. The thought of the prisoner being freed and allowed to go to his sister—which I was certain he did not have—was dangerously attractive to me. Perhaps, I thought, Buckley was right. What Nguyen was doing to the boy was relatively bloodless, but evil. I was too tired to think clearly about it any longer. My head had begun to pound. Whatever Buckley's motive was for wanting a quick end to the interrogation, mine was a simple desire to sleep, and maybe, a little, a desire to see the boy sleep.

McGruder, who had been watching us since he had heard

me speak his name, stood up. He crossed the room with a deliberate step and sat down heavily next to me. With Buckley on one side and with McGruder's square, pockmarked face on the other, I tried to pull myself up. But I was too tired. Something was happening inside me. My heart was pounding and I could feel the veins thick in every part of my body. I had not rested for more than twenty hours. There had been the work on the beach, the thirst, the waiting in the blazing sun in the stockade yard, the mind-killing sounds of the interrogation. Now there was no one to look to for help. Nguyen was interested only in the prisoner, and pretended not to see the three of us together. Even Finley, who had trusted me before, was watching me now as though I, too, filled him with a nameless horror.

McGruder was even more impatient than Buckley. He had been quiet since he had returned to the room at sunset, except for his harmless outburst at Nguyen, but now with Buckley watching Nguyen with a new look of distrust, his hope had revived.

"You're still letting him off, Lieutenant," he muttered, fixing his eyes between the boy's shoulder blades, as if he could see Buckley's eyes reflected there.

"We're simply letting Sergeant Nguyen have his way," Buckley murmured, turning his head slightly toward me, then turning away, as if to say that it was I, and not he, who was responsible.

McGruder swore and looked past me at Buckley. "Give the kid a forty-five and he'll kill every man in this room. This is a Viet Cong terrorist, Lieutenant," he said; "this is the enemy!"

Buckley nodded in agreement, which caused McGruder to turn to me as the only remaining obstacle. I hated him, and

I feared him. Once, in my platoon, I'd had one like him. The Army was his license to kill, without reason. Yet the force of his will was more than I could fight against, now that Buckley had stepped out of his way. My face was hot. I was sweating and weak.

"You don't know that," I said, but I kept my eyes fixed on Nguyen so that I would not have to look directly at McGruder. "He may be only what he says he is—a boy who picked up the grenades to protect himself until he could sell them in Saigon."

"He was going to give the money to his sister," McGruder sneered.

"It's possible."

He laughed, as if he had trapped me. "You know what the girls are in Saigon. If she's there, she's a whore."

"That's beside the point. The fact remains that we have no way of knowing why the boy was carrying the grenades or where he was going. It's no use acting as though we do."

"Hell, man!" McGruder cried. "He was caught red-handed on his way to the guerrillas!"

"That's a reasonable suspicion, nothing more."

"Shut your mouth, jailbird! I've been in this war since the day it started. I learned about my Vietnamese the hard way, and you ain't gonna tell me a thing!"

McGruder had grabbed my open collar. The material was rotten from sweat and dirt and it ripped away, but still he held me by what was left. I wanted to make him take his hands off me, but I remembered in time that he was a sergeant and I was a convict, in faded khaki. My eyes were burning with fatigue. I looked away. Only when I hated him did I remember that I had once been an officer and that it had been good.

"Let him go," Buckley said, and McGruder released his grip.

For a second my stomach was sick, and I thought I would have to lean over and vomit.

"Are you all right?" Buckley asked.

"I'm okay," I said.

He told McGruder to keep his place, and not to use his hands on me again. But it was clear that he and McGruder understood one another. Still, when I sat up McGruder grunted an apology to me.

"I came in at Danang before anybody else got into this stinkin' mess," he said, in a voice that was almost a voice of reason. "I've seen our kids knocked to pieces by Malaysian gates and stuck through the chest in punji pits. Believe me, Lieutenant, this little devil that we've got knows every trick in their book. You let him go and he'll make a point of killing you inside a week." He looked at me for a moment, then he added, "Now you think about that when you start feeling sorry for the little son of a bitch."

I shook my head, wanting only to be left alone, for I knew that McGruder was right as far as his knowledge went. "But the kid is helpless," I said.

McGruder spit at the floor. He was determined to have his way and I had nothing with which to defend either myself or the boy, for I wanted nothing but to sleep.

Buckley leaned forward to support McGruder. "He isn't helpless if you put him behind a thirty-caliber machine gun. Listen, Kreuger," he said, dropping his voice to an angry whisper, "this is our chance! These little bastards have been ambushing us and getting away with it. The villagers help them. No one's on our side out here. If we don't help each other, we're lost." He looked at me for a moment, squinting into the light, then he said, "If you aren't going to help us, at least you have no right to stand in our way!"

Only then did I realize that both of them had been asking for my consent, as if they could not go on without it. I had no power, except the language, which they would need if they had their way. I could consent to nothing. Yet they were thrusting some unwanted influence upon me, and, slowly, I saw that the more of us who shared the responsibility for whatever it was that they wanted to do in that room, the less any of us could be held accountable for later when the reckoning came to be made. There could be no talk of guilt if everyone was an accomplice.

"Leave me out of it," I said.

Buckley once again laid his hand on my shoulder. "I have special orders from the major," he said, and then added in a quiet voice, "If we get the information out of the kid you won't go back to the stockade."

I waited for a moment, watching him. All that I could see was his forehead, which was caught in the light. His face was sweating.

He shifted his position when I didn't answer, and began again. "I'm telling you exactly what my orders are, Kreuger," he said. "You'll get a full reinstatement to rank. They'll put you on the staff. Believe me, it can be done. There will be red tape and a delay because it will have to go up to division, but the major knows what he's talking about when he says the C.G. will approve it. He was your convening authority. That's all you need. They'll billet you with the officers here, very quietly, until it goes through. But," he added, "first you have to cooperate with us."

For a moment I didn't move. A great weight seemed to have been lifted from me. I felt light, though my head ached worse than ever. I thought that I would hit Buckley in the face, to end it now and to be sent back to the silence of the sand dunes where a man could forget everything that had ever happened to him. My hands felt as though they had been urinated on.

Buckley was smiling at me confidently. "The major is in a hurry," he said, and gave me a look of complicity that I had never seen before. Even McGruder managed an expression of dim comradeship on his stonelike face. I stood up to get away from them and walked around the table, past Nguyen and the boy, and sat down unsteadily on an empty cot. My body ached too much to move any further. I wanted Cowley or Finley to sit by me now, but they only stared at me from a distance and would not come near.

Still Buckley was smiling hungrily, as though he had understood nothing at all. Then, as if by arrangement between the three of us, he and McGruder stood up together and moved slowly to either side of the table. McGruder took Nguyen by the arm and drew him to one side without a sound. Their motions seemed effortless, irresistible. It might all have been a dream. Cowley watched them and moved carefully back against the farthest wall. Nguyen kept his balance when McGruder pushed him away, and he stood staring at them from outside the circle of light; but he said nothing. Finley covered his ears, as though the sudden silence was unbearable—but I was aware of only an irrational surge of pleasure when the sound of Nguyen's voice was cut off in mid-sentence. The boy looked up unsteadily, perplexed, as if waking from a dream and looking for the source from which that thunderous silence had come down on him. And then I saw McGruder, towering over him, blocking the light, reaching out his big hand and taking the boy by the throat, while he slowly drew his other hand, clenched in a massive fist, up under the boy's face. I did not move from my cot. I was paralyzed. I wanted to shout that this was not what I had meant, that this was not what I had wanted—but my head was throbbing, my arms had grown weak, and suddenly I realized that I had the typhoid in my veins. Someone in the room was laughing insanely. I sat with the fever in me and watched as McGruder turned his fist this way and that in the light, forcing the boy to look at the flat knuckles. Then the laughter stopped. I was cold and shivering inside. Nguyen made a short cry of protest and stepped into the light, but he was afraid. There was nothing to be done. I only wished that they would hurry. McGruder ignored Nguyen and drew his fist a few inches away from the boy's head—no farther than that—and then brought it back against his skull. The blow was slow and effortless, but the boy was knocked off his feet and hurtled to the ground.

Then Nguyen came to life and began to scream. "If you had not let go of his neck you would have killed him!" he cried.

McGruder nodded, looking impassively down at the boy, who lay on his side with his face in the dirt. McGruder was calm now. His arms hung quietly at his sides. It was Nguyen who had lost control of himself and was shouting.

Buckley crushed out his cigarette and came into the circle of light. "Finley," he said, "fix the prisoner."

But Finley would not move out of his corner, and Nguyen rushed to Buckley, still thinking that he could stop them.

"I told you what would happen if you hurt him!" he cried. "You see, already he has escaped! Sergeant McGruder knows *nothing.*"

He glared at McGruder over Buckley's shoulder, but McGruder remained stolidly planted under the light as if defying anyone to take his place away from him.

"I have worked for many hours," Nguyen pleaded. "The prisoner is growing weak. Do not ruin everything now. There is no reason for this!"

The appeal to Buckley was futile. He simply repeated his order to Finley, who glanced up at me. Then, when he saw that there was no help for him, he dragged himself to his feet and went to the boy. He turned him over on his back. The arms and legs fell over with the heavy limpness of the dead. Finley began to examine him. When the boy's face was in the light I could see that McGruder's seemingly effortless blow had torn the flesh away from the left side of his cheek beneath the eye. The high cheekbone was laid bare. It protruded like a bloody tooth. Finley gave him an injection, and the boy's ribs began to rise and fall as his respiration increased. For a moment all of us looked down at him in silence, waiting for his eyes to open in the hard light, fascinated.

"Put him on his feet," Buckley ordered.

"Wait," Nguyen said, raising his face. He looked at McGruder, then at Buckley, and with the quickness of a professional he reconciled himself to the change in their temper. "If you are going to do this," he said in a subdued voice, "you must do it properly. It is more difficult than you imagine. I also have much experience in physical compulsion. Above all," he added, glancing at McGruder, "we must not damage the head."

Nguyen seemed concerned only to keep his control over the boy, at any cost. It was McGruder whom he feared, not Buckley. McGruder looked at him threateningly, but Buckley was eager to agree.

"Good, now we'll finish this," he said, and he told Mc-Gruder to stand out of the light and to let Nguyen—he again called him Sergeant Nguyen—regain his place.

But then Nguyen turned to me, as if he dreaded the circle of light, and realized for the first time that I was in the room and that Buckley had called me "lieutenant." For a second his eyes lit with the hope that we could prevent it, if we stood together.

"Lieutenant Kreuger?" he asked, resting his eyes on me questioningly, waiting.

I could feel the eyes of everyone in the room fixed upon me—Buckley's with a cold look of warning, McGruder's smoldering, Nguyen's dark eyes with his silent question deep within them, and the eyes of Finley, wide, frightened, bruised with fatigue. I wondered if the prisoner was watching me too, and if he understood.

I tried to think, but I could think of nothing. None of them seemed to understand that I was powerless. All that I wanted was to keep out of it, and to sleep. My head was beating painfully, my arms ached, I was weak—and I leaned back against the blistering wall and closed my eyes.

CHAPTER *FOUR*

IT WAS TWELVE-THIRTY, midnight.

I would willingly have slept, if I had been able to sleep, for my body remained heavy with the fever. Sounds were lost to me, or magnified at sudden moments into alarming shouts, which, when I raised my eyes, proved to be no more than Buckley's voice or Nguyen threatening the prisoner. In my tent I could have slept and the fever would have been mildly pleasant. Here it was only dulling and painful. Instead of being horrified at what was happening, I felt peevish. Colors, too, were blurred and then made brilliant in an erratic way as my pulse rose and fell. But there was little color in the room to disturb my eyes. Everything was black, like the shadows and the boy's pajamas, or gray tin, or khaki, or so glaring in the electric light that it seemed to be a pallid white. Only the knife and the little wounds on the prisoner's groin were red; but even that dried quickly in the heat and was baked to a dull brick color. Finally the room was uninteresting. My mind, attacked by the serum, kept trying to escape.

It was Buckley who made escape impossible. He stood on one side of the metal table, gripping its hard corners with his hands, tense and excited now that he had turned the interrogation in the direction that he wanted it to go, glancing eagerly from Nguyen and back to me, as though I were his accomplice. He and Nguyen talked in low tones. For a moment they argued. Then they came to an understanding and both of them turned around and faced the boy. They were ready to begin.

"Tell him that the talking is over," Buckley said eagerly. "Make him understand what will happen to him now if he doesn't confess."

He spoke as if he were confident that at this threat of greater pain the boy's resistance would collapse, though it had held firm under nine hours of hard questioning. I was sure that it would not. Still, my faith in Buckley rose, a little; I hoped that he had intended to use physical torture as only a threat, which would suffice in itself through simple terror.

But Nguyen knew better. He startled all of us by screaming the warning in the prisoner's face. I sat up, alert. Nguyen had braced his feet and looked as though he intended to carry out the threat whether it was necessary or not, for the sheer pleasure of it. It was the reverse of his previous manner with the boy. Now, instead of trying to numb him, he seemed to want to shock him. No doubt it cost him a good deal of hidden anger to discard the fruits of his interrogation. Once he glanced down at me as if I were to blame; and I could see that he, too, had mistaken my abstention for consent. It seemed impossible to make myself understood in that room. But the mistake had been made. It was useless to protest now. I only hoped that it would be over quickly, and without too much bloodshed.

At first the boy was bewildered. He blinked and frowned at Nguyen, for the words that Nguyen now used were not those that he had grown accustomed to hearing. They seemed to have no meaning for him.

*98*

"You will confess everything or we will torture you!" Nguyen screamed. "You will confess now! There will be no second chance!"

Then the boy understood, and he seemed to shrink physically, as if to defend himself by becoming smaller and more compact—but he did not make a sound. I felt the same apprehension that I had felt earlier when I had seen that his face would register pain. Now he should have been brave under the threat of torture. Or, if he was a coward, he should have confessed, and so spared us all. But he was neither brave nor prudent; he was simply obstinate.

Nguyen held up the full length of his short blade. He had kept all but the tip hidden before, but now he turned it this way and that in front of the prisoner's eyes, making it flash in the light.

"I will cut you with this if you do not speak," he whispered, pressing his face so close to the boy's that they nearly touched. Now his tone of voice jarred my nerves more than the grinding monotony of the interrogation had. I did not see how any of us, least of all the boy, could stand it for long. Even Buckley was suddenly unnerved. We watched the prisoner's face for some sign of surrender, but the face was rigid and expressionless.

"Very well," Nguyen said in a businesslike way, and thrust the tip of the blade into one of the small wounds that the interrogation had left on the boy's groin. He stuck it in with a steady hand, accurately and swiftly—and then he turned the handle clockwise and withdrew it with a flip upward of the point. The boy's hands had been tied behind his back again.

He could not protect himself. His mouth opened, but no sound came out. It was over before any of us realized what had happened.

Then my heart began to pound. I thought that I would cry out or that I would use my fists, but I seemed paralyzed, and could do nothing. Buckley's face had gone ash-white and he was leaning forward over the edge of the table, holding it with his fingers, staring at Nguyen and then at the knife, which was just slightly blooded on the tip.

"My God," he whispered, "you didn't give him a chance!"

Nguyen turned deliberately to him with an evil look in his eyes. "I am doing only what you wanted," he said coldly.

"I didn't tell you to stab him! I wanted you to give him enough time to realize that we mean business. He'll confess if he sees he has no other way out."

Nguyen laid the knife carefully down on the table within his reach. "It will do no good to threaten him if he does not have a reason to believe us. Perhaps you wish to use the knife?"

Buckley shook his head. "No," he said, straightening up and stepping back from the table. He took a deep breath. "Ask him if he's ready to talk now," he said, and rubbed his eyes and forehead, which seemed to restore him a little.

Nguyen turned slowly back to the boy. He seemed to be enjoying showing Buckley the ultimate application of his own logic. Suddenly he lunged forward and screamed in the boy's face. "Will you tell us now? Or do you want me to use the knife again? I will stick you in the same place each time, only deeper, until I am inside your belly! Where were you told to meet your comrades?"

The boy closed his eyes and refused to say anything.

Nguyen picked up the knife, allowing the blade to slide across the surface of the metal table. The sound was like steel being sharpened. He looked at Buckley, who fixed his eyes despairingly on the boy's face.

"Go ahead," Buckley said weakly, "but be careful."

"I know what to do, Lieutenant," Nguyen replied acidly, and instantly stabbed the boy in the same wound, with the same twisting motion. I saw the prisoner's head jerk to one side and his jaw snap shut, and I turned away.

Cowley was standing near the tool crib, his eyes narrowed and menacing, ready to fight, as if he felt some irrational fear for his own safety; and I noticed for the first time that the heavy tools were potential weapons. Finley was crouched on the floor nearby. He had covered his face with his hands. Now and then he made little whimpering sounds, as if he were in pain. When he saw me watching him he got up and came to me. "They're crazy," he whispered in a girl's voice. "They've gone crazy, Lieutenant. You've got to stop them."

"Shut up," I said.

He looked at me hopelessly and sat down with his head in his hands. His knees were drawn up under his chin. I envied him. Suddenly I wanted to begin rubbing my face too, but I resisted.

Soon the knife was in constant use. Each time that Nguyen shouted for confession, he stabbed. The little bruises left on the boy's groin were punctured one by one. Each became a running wound. Still the boy would not speak. His only response was to roll his head from side to side and to open and close his mouth as if he could not breathe. I began to hate the sight of him. With every thrust of the knife, and with every cry of Nguyen's voice, the room was filled with a silent scream of pain. The metallic sound of it echoed off the walls like a siren. We did not hear it. We felt it.

Buckley had moved around the table in front of the prisoner where he could watch the effect of the knife on his flesh. Perhaps he only wanted to keep Nguyen from hurting him too badly; or, now that he was past the first shock of the knife, he might have wanted to see what it was like. It was impossible to say. The rest of us wanted only to hide. Even Nguyen was growing tense. His attention became so riveted on the boy that he seemed to have forgotten about the rest of us. The verbal interrogation had required patience and endurance; this new work seemed to require rage, which was exhausting. The back of his shirt became stained with sweat. The muscles in his neck and jaw that were normally invisible stood out like wire cable. Only McGruder continued to move about the room without watching the knife. Something was at work inside him. It would not let him stand still. He was breathing with as much difficulty as the prisoner, though he was not being cut. But finally even he stopped and stood awkwardly at one side of the table, watching the rise and fall of the knife.

It went on for an hour, without relief for either the prisoner or for us, and then Nguyen had to stop. He was breathless. He stepped back from the light to rest his eyes and explained to us that it was necessary to keep from puncturing the wall of the gut.

"We must cause him the most pain without allowing him to die," he gasped, and closed his eyes for a moment. "There are many other ways."

"What are you going to do?" Buckley asked, frowning, though whether it was because Nguyen had stopped or because he was going to continue, I could not tell.

*102*

Nguyen laid the knife carefully aside and said that for the time being, the groin was worn out. He waited for a moment, then went on. "He feels very little pain there now," he said. "It is numb. We must turn him around and use the back." He added, as if to reassure us all, that the boy was very strong-willed, but that he would prevent his getting away. He seemed obsessed with the idea that the boy should go on living, but now—I did not know why—I hated him for it, though I did not want the boy to die either.

McGruder was swearing, at the walls and at Nguyen, generally. When it became irritating Buckley told him to shut up. Nguyen wanted an assistant, and Buckley ordered Cowley to come to the table. Cowley did not move, except to edge backwards still farther from the circle of light and nearer the tool crib, where there were hammers and wrenches. Buckley did not waste time arguing with him. He told Finley to do it instead, but Finley was too withdrawn to move. He seemed to be asleep. Then Buckley became furious. He ordered McGruder, who was moving ominously toward Cowley, to go outside and get Russell.

I glanced up at the door, hating to have Russell enter the room. He would have no reason to suspect anything and would not resist. Somehow I did not want him to see it. But Nguyen looked down at me and asked me if I would rather hold the prisoner's wrists across the table myself. He was vengeful. I saw that he had not reconciled himself to the loss of his interrogation, and that he blamed me for it. I ignored him, though I should have defended myself, and Russell was brought in.

"Leave your carbine and ammunition belt outside," Nguyen ordered. "We must have no firearms in the room.

That way there is no fear of the prisoner attacking us, since he cannot hurt us with his hands."

Russell obediently dropped his equipment outside the door and stood just beyond the circle of light. I could see his trousers and his boots, but not his face. No doubt he was staring at the bloodstains, and at the knife. I knew that Finley and I looked haggard, sitting together in the farthest corner of the room, but I didn't give a damn what Russell thought.

Nguyen took the time to explain what lay ahead, now that he had acquired an assistant whom he outranked and who, presumably, would be at his complete use to dispose of as he chose. He spoke as if addressing a student. I was glad that I could not see Russell's eyes.

"Our method is a crude and therefore a simple one," Nguyen said, looking at McGruder, then back at Russell. "The prisoner is being made to give us his information by the certainty of pain, without release of any kind. Skill is required, but I am trained. The only danger is losing self-control and inflicting a mortal injury without confession. Remember," he said, glancing around the room at all of us, "that we are his enemy, and that he knows now that he can only defeat us by dying. Therefore we must see to it that he lives."

Russell's boots did not move, but his hands, black and slender, graceful hands, dropped down into the light and hung helplessly at his sides.

McGruder slammed the table with his fist. "You're still letting him off!" he shouted. "You're playing with him. You can't make him talk with that little knife. Hurt him, really hurt him once, for Christ sake, and he'll talk! You're cutting him for the fun of it."

"You will see that I know far better than you how to hurt

him," Nguyen answered coldly. He had lost one part of his control over the prisoner's fate—the slow questioning. Now he had to prove his willingness to inflict injury upon him, or he would lose what little remained. Above all, Nguyen seemed to want to stay with the boy, no matter how much he had to hurt him.

"We will begin on the small of the back," he said, turning to Russell. "Then, if he does not confess, we will work our way up the sides, along the ribs. After that there are the insides of the arms, the fat of the thighs, the armpits, and the scrotum. There is enough for what we need," he said, and assured us that pain in any of the areas that he had named was particularly hard to bear. "But he will not last that long," he added, gazing at the boy's face, which was already lined and bloodless. Again he warned Russell to avoid broken bones or a cut that went too deep and bled too much, as if Russell were the tormentor. Russell seemed not to hear.

"God*damit*," McGruder said wearily, "why don't you get it over with?"

Nguyen ignored him, but turned to Buckley. "Do not allow him to touch the prisoner again."

Buckley told McGruder to keep away, and he moved back. "I don't want any part of it," McGruder muttered, and began to go to his cot. But suddenly he turned around and pounded the table again until the knife, lying on its metal edge, was rattling up and down. "I don't trust all this talk!" he shouted, glaring at Nguyen. "What's it gotten us?"

"Get out of the way," Buckley said. "We're going to let Sergeant Nguyen show us what he can do."

McGruder clenched his fists and backed away, but he said nothing more. Then Buckley turned to Nguyen with his hands

**105**

on his hips, and said, "Only let me warn you that if you can't make him talk you'll be replaced, and I won't be responsible for what will happen then."

"We are wasting time," Nguyen replied, and turned summarily to Russell. "You will hold his wrists across the table, please."

Then he told the boy to turn around, and cut the cord that bound his wrists. The thin hands instantly cupped themselves over the groin, where the flesh was torn. He was slow in turning, for his legs were swollen and stiff from the hours of standing on the hard floor without moving. When he was finally facing the table Nguyen pushed him forward at the waist until the boy's chin rose instinctively to avoid the metal surface. Again Nguyen told Russell to take his wrists, but Russell did not move. I could see his black hands still hanging lifelessly at his sides. Slowly he seemed to have understood what was going to happen in the room. Buckley had to reach forward and hold the boy's arms down, for they were moving freely over the table, as if searching for something.

"Do what you're told, soldier!" he shouted at Russell.

Russell made an involuntary motion forward, then stopped again. McGruder was on his feet, eager to use his hands on Russell, and I saw Cowley start for McGruder with a hammer in his clenched fist. At first I didn't understand, but when I looked at Cowley's face I saw that he had gone mad and was going to kill McGruder if he laid a hand on Russell. Fortunately, before he could do anything, Russell had encircled his obedient fingers around the boy's thin wrists. It was a mechanical grip, lifeless, like a death lock, but it stopped McGruder and he turned back to his cot, satisfied that Buckley's orders were being carried out. Cowley recovered himself in time and

*106*

moved unsteadily back. No one else had seen him, and I had not made a sound.

"That is good," Nguyen said quietly, studying the boy's position with a practiced eye. "Draw the arms forward a little more, please."

Russell did it, until the boy's back and shoulders were stretched out as far as they could go. When the muscles were strained sufficiently Nguyen seemed satisfied and nodded.

In his new position, bent over the table, the prisoner's backbone and ribs stood out clearly in the light. There seemed little flesh on his spare body, but then Nguyen picked up the knife and began to flick it lightly over his skin, as if testing it —and I saw that there was enough. Soon the knife moved more slowly and went in deeper, and I understood at last that it made no difference which of them, Nguyen or McGruder, had his way with the prisoner. Perhaps Nguyen's method was worse. He wanted to prevent the death of the boy, for whatever reason, but he was slow and deliberate. None of us could keep out of it, for we were forced to watch without protest for too long to remain innocent. McGruder's instincts had the advantage of anger and would put a quick end to the business. There seemed less guilt in that for all of us, though, of course, the boy could not be expected to survive. It is possible that in all of our minds the unspoken wish for the prisoner's death had found a place. In my imagination I saw him lying on the table, as if sleeping, but I did not know if he was dead or alive. Perhaps it was only myself that I saw. I wondered if any of us would find sleep while the boy lived.

It was not likely. It seemed impossible that we could watch what Nguyen was doing to the boy's back with the knife, yet I could not tear my eyes away. I had never seen human flesh cut—not, at least, at such close quarters. Nguyen was nibbling at the muscles above the hip, over the kidneys, with slow twisting motions of the blade. At first the flesh resisted, for it was lean and hard; but then it yielded and the knife suddenly penetrated. Nguyen screamed out his demand for confession. The boy's head tried to come up, his sides tightened, rippled with pain, then relaxed, and tightened again—but he remained silent. Once Nguyen had turned the blade the opened flesh cut easily, as if its surface resistance had been destroyed, or because the edge of the knife was sharper than the point. Nguyen tried to take a little piece of flesh with the knife each time he flipped it out. Sometimes he succeeded, and a little hole, red and bleeding, would be left. At other times a flap of skin would remain, and cover the wound. Yet the flesh was living and warm and tried to fight back. Even the deep cuts seemed to slowly close themselves, though they continued to bleed.

Nguyen went on screaming and stabbing. It seemed incredible that he could prevent himself from thrusting the blade all the way in, to a fatal depth. But he only jabbed and punctured with perfect control. Still the boy was silent. McGruder sat on his cot with his hands covering his head, stamping his foot each time Nguyen shouted.

Then Russell, who had been staring at the boy's uplifted face, suddenly let go of his wrists and vomited. He had time to turn away from the table and bend over to heave it up on the floor, in front of Buckley. It kept coming. Then he began gagging, though there was nothing left, as if he would throw up the lining of his stomach. He retched dry for a long time. I thought he was going into convulsions; but finally he

*108*

stopped, and his spasms became a simple trembling. He leaned against the wall, moaning.

"He's going to pass out," Finley whispered, raising his eyes barely enough to peer over his forearms at Russell.

Buckley was swearing furiously. He looked as though he were going to use his fists on Russell, but he controlled himself and shouted at Finley to clean up the pool of vomit. "Get a bucket of water in here!" he cried. "It stinks like hell."

Finley shook his head. He didn't look as if he could stand up.

"Get up, you bastard!" Buckley shouted, and rushed at him as if he were going to kick him to his feet.

Finley gave a little cry of despair—like a small animal in a trap—and half rose, but Cowley stepped in front of him and shoved him back on the cot. "I'll clean it up," he said. Buckley stared at him as though he had forgotten that he was in the room, but he didn't argue; and Cowley walked past Russell, who was still shaking too hard to help him, and went out of the hut.

Still Nguyen was screaming at the prisoner. The knife was still in use. From the top of the boy's buttocks to the middle of his back there was an irregular stitch of red wounds, each a demand for confession, and each a stubborn refusal. Apparently neither Nguyen nor the prisoner was aware of Russell's sickness. The boy's arms remained motionless on the table as if they could no longer move. But suddenly McGruder lunged to his feet and leaned into the light, staring wildly into the boy's face. His mouth was so twisted with hate that I expected to hear him emit some animal roar of anger, or perhaps of madness—but he remained speechless, as if it was some look on the boy's face itself that had drawn him to his feet. One would have thought that the boy was laughing, or weeping, to have made McGruder so furious. But I could only see the back of his head.

Buckley was circling the room with his hands driven deep into his pockets, like an animal trainer. With every cry from Nguyen he threw his head back as if it were he, and not the boy, who was stabbed. He paced behind McGruder, whose big hands had now locked themselves around the prisoner's slender wrists, and he stopped each time in front of Russell's mess, went back the other way, stopped, and returned to it again.

We were going mad. All of us. Suddenly I pictured the camp outside, the silence of the bay at night, the lights that shined under the quiet doors of other huts—and I saw the five of us as we really were. I stood up, in spite of my fever and weakness, and grabbed Buckley by the elbow.

"You've got to stop this," I whispered hoarsely. "Can't you see what's happening?"

Buckley looked at me without hearing. He opened his mouth, as if awakening from a nightmare, but at that moment the room was filled with an unearthly wail. The prisoner had thrown his head violently to one side and made his first cry of pain, a sustained scream that contained all that he had held back for hours, and which went on until his lungs were empty, as though he would not permit himself to cry out again and was making what he could of his momentary release.

Everyone in the room froze. We listened. The knife was suspended in mid-air. Even McGruder backed away uncertainly and sat down, peering at the boy's face. I could see only that the jaw was open as wide as it would go, nearly unhinged,

*110*

and that it remained open though no further sound came out. There was no breath remaining in the body. He seemed to want to die. But then he could stand it no longer, and he inhaled, a long, shuddering inrush of air, life-giving, hateful, that made him drop his head. Again his back was exposed to Nguyen, who instantly recovered himself. The knife came up with a flash. The boy's head snapped upright, and Nguyen cried out once more for confession.

The room had returned to normal. Buckley looked at me and jerked his arm out of my grip. "We are not going to stop it," he said quietly, summoning all of his strength. "We are going through with it now no matter how long it takes. By God, Kreuger, we're going to make him talk!"

"You're only going to kill him," I said, pursuing him around the table.

"We've gone too far to stop now," he answered, facing me. "Besides, it's Nguyen who's doing it. It's his method, not ours."

"I don't care whose method it is, you can't go on with it!"

"What do you want then? Do you think we can go back to the questioning after this? Don't be a fool."

"Then let McGruder have the boy! Get it over with, if this is what you wanted."

A look of menace came into Buckley's eyes, and he said, "You wanted it too, Kreuger. We asked you. You didn't say a word to stop it."

"I didn't want this!"

"What then? What did you think it was going to be?" he demanded. "You knew the kid wasn't going to talk."

McGruder had risen to his feet again. The air was filled with the insane sounds of Nguyen's voice and the stench of

Russell's vomit. My strength was gone, and I felt sick. I could hardly stand. The typhoid was still pounding in my veins. My head ached with fever. I stopped short in front of Buckley, wondering why I was shouting at him in the center of the room, so far from where I belonged.

"I thought it would be over quicker than this," I murmured.

Buckley took me by the arm as though I were an invalid and led me back to my cot. "It will be," he assured me. "We won't let this go on a minute longer than we have to. But, Kreuger," he added, in a voice of reason against which I no longer had a defense, "we have no choice. It's this or nothing now. You have to keep your nerve. Come on," he said, speaking like a good friend, "rest for a while. Go outside and get some air, if you have to. You'll feel better, and you'll see that we're right."

I sat down and shook my head. "I won't agree to any more of it."

Buckley stood over me then, threateningly. All that I saw were his knees and—across the top of the table, again holding the boy's wrists—the well-lit face of McGruder, watching us.

"Don't buck me, Kreuger," he warned. "There are things worse than the sand dunes. The major is backing me. There's no one in this room can tell me what to do, and there's nothing that will keep me from getting what I need out of this little bastard. You're going to have to do your part, whether you like it or not."

I was too exhausted to look up at him. He wanted something, though I did not know what. I wanted nothing but to sleep. It was an unequal battle, and my anger abandoned me.

Buckley took my lowered head for a sign of assent. I no longer cared. All that I wanted now was rest, or, if I could find a way, escape. I longed to be in my tent inside the stockade fence again, with Cowley and Smith, waiting for the morning floodlights to come on.

But then my eyes were drawn to Nguyen. The room had become totally silent. The only voices had been Buckley's and my own, and then, as though we had all gone stone-deaf, there were none. It was impossible to avoid his eyes. Again they were filled with the silent question that I had seen two hours before. I looked at the ribs of the boy, gleaming with sweat under the light. Absurd as it seemed, I knew then that Nguyen was the boy's sole protector, for the ribs were still unmarked and free of pain—and Nguyen was asking me, again, to help him fight Buckley so that they could stay that way.

Cowley came in with a bucket of water and a shovel. Buckley made Russell help him scoop his own vomit outside, away from the door, and then to flush the dirt floor until nothing remained but a puddle of mud.

"We'd better leave the door open," Cowley said.

Buckley refused, though the smell hung thickly in the room. He seemed only then to realize that he had allowed Cowley, who knew what was happening in the hut, to go freely through the camp. He ordered the door closed and locked.

"If there's a break in our security, soldier, I'll come down on you so you never forget it."

Cowley only nodded, as if nothing could frighten him anymore, and he took Russell to one side of the room, where he would be out of the way.

Nguyen gave me a final look of appeal. I did not respond. I did not move.

"Very well," he said, as if speaking to himself, and he turned around and began to work the knife between the boy's ribs to show me the consequences of my refusal, and to punish me.

I got off my cot, unable to stand it any longer. Two hours of torture had achieved nothing, except to show us that we were more vicious and more cunning—all of us—than we had known. I felt as if I were already buried up to my chest in scalding sand, with nothing more to lose. There was no way out, and nothing left for any of us now but to fight or go under.

CHAPTER *FIVE*

I DISCOVERED that one could sleep, in spite of everything. I did not know whether to be grateful or ashamed, but I found that I was not alone. When I opened my eyes I saw Nguyen bending over the boy, who now lay face-up on the table, staring into the light. I was on my cot with my head resting against the wooden frame. When I moved I was stiff and my left arm was numb, but I managed to sit up. The folded newspaper had formed a painful lump in my pocket. I took it out and threw it under my cot.

Finley and Russell were lying huddled close together on the floor. Buckley was on the cot next to mine with his back and shoulders hunched against the wall. His head had fallen awkwardly to one side. He looked as though his neck had been broken, but I supposed that he was only asleep. Even McGruder had collapsed, and was snoring fitfully across the room. I had no idea how much time had passed, or whether it was night or day.

Cowley was awake too, and he was watching me. He rose stealthily, as though he had been waiting for such an opportunity, and crossed the room and sat next to me.

"I don't see how the hell you could sleep," he said.

I shrugged and started to answer, but Cowley leaned closer to me with a burning expression in his usually dull eyes.

"Listen to me," he whispered; "we've got to get out of this."

I asked him what he meant, and he said that the two of us

had to escape before Buckley or McGruder woke up and the interrogation began again. He promised that he could handle the sentries, particularly, he said, as it was still dark outside. I asked him where he thought we could go, and he said the Delta or the Cambodian border.

"You're out of your mind," I told him, and he admitted that he hadn't given it much thought.

"We've got to get out of here," he muttered; "then we can figure out what to do."

The idea struck me as a joke; and it occurred to me, for some reason, that I did not know what Cowley had done to get himself sent to Quai Dong in the first place. I asked him. He looked at me without understanding what I had said. Then he frowned and told me that he had knocked his lieutenant's teeth out in a Saigon bar—and at that he became embarrassed, in spite of his preoccupation with escape, for he knew that I had been a lieutenant—and he blinked.

Every man in the camp knew. Probably a guard had let the word out on the day of my arrival. I could remember that on my first morning in the food line I had overheard a man behind me whisper to his companion that the Army "had busted some smart lieutenant's ass" and sent him to Quai Dong. That had been Smith. I was the subject of general amusement for a week; then, when they saw that I was just another prisoner and that I did my work, they let it alone.

"Kreuger!" Cowley whispered impatiently. "Did you hear me?"

I collected my thoughts with an effort, and told him that I had.

"Are you with me, or not?" he asked.

I looked at him. He was stupid—obviously, he was even

more stupid that I had known—but he was my friend and I did not want to laugh at him.

"No," I said, and then I tried to make him understand. "Look, they'll shoot you down before you get out of the maintenance yard. Don't you realize that there are three fences to get through? And even if you got away, you don't have anywhere to go but Quai Dong."

Cowley wouldn't listen. He was angry and said that he had counted on me to help him, for I would have known a way of escape if anyone would, but that I had let him down.

"I'll look out for myself from now on," he said, and he stood up and recrossed the room, where he began to sulk or to make new plans, it was difficult to tell which.

Watching Cowley's heavy face made me uncomfortable. I moved to the door, thinking that he was going to get himself killed. There was no reason for him to hate the room badly enough to want to risk his life to get away from it; though, when it came to that, I hated the room badly enough myself. No one hated it more. But I hated it because it was a threat to our survival, and Cowley was only making it more dangerous than it had been. There was no gain for any of us in that, and therefore it was stupid.

When I stepped outside the hut the air was cool. I breathed in the refreshing smell of the invisible sea and felt my sleep coming back, only comforting now, more like true sleep than exhaustion. The camp was still hidden in darkness, but it was nearly daybreak, for the horizon showed the black silhouette of the hills against the sky. It was more than starlight—the sun was on its way. Everything was perfectly silent. In that slowly dissolving blackness I could make out the dark coils of barbed wire that surrounded the hut. For some reason

I feared them less now that I would soon be able to see them. Even the glare of the electric bulb, which fell on the ground in front of the doorway, was enfeebled by that vague promise of light.

I saw Cowley watching me suspiciously through the open door, sitting on his cot with the hard light falling across his brooding face. I went around to the corner of the entanglement to get away from him and looked toward the bay. The floodlights were turned on inside the prison stockade; therefore it was already past four-thirty. They made a single pool of distant light, the only clearly visible thing in the darkness, in which tiny formations of convicts were standing in rows, marshaled like morning insects. Beyond the stockade the sea was murmuring quietly in the stillness. Then I heard the faint metallic bark of the loudspeakers. They were giving work orders for the day. I had been on that beach the day before, though now it seemed irreconcilably far away. Still, I told myself that only one night had passed and that, really, nothing had happened. With any luck at all I would be there again tomorrow, or even that afternoon, if the sun came up, digging in the sand next to Smith—somehow I did not picture Cowley there with us now, for he seemed one of the dead—assured once more that nothing could happen to me. We might even get to work with our feet in the cool water around the LST. My sleep had driven the fever out of my head, and I swore that if I could get back to the beach I would never leave it again.

"Is it morning?" Nguyen asked quietly when I reentered the room.

"Yes," I said, "it's nearly dawn."

He nodded, and seemed grateful to me for telling him. His

*120*

face was sunken with fatigue, but he did not take his eyes off the boy. He was speaking in his relentless whisper, telling him to confess, and to sleep. Probably he had spent the entire night alone by the table, bending solicitously over the prisoner to keep him from closing his eyes and escaping for even a moment of sleep. The boy was trying painfully to answer. The knife lay on the table within Nguyen's reach, but when I looked at it I saw that the stains on the blade were not fresh.

"Did he rest?" I asked, moving around to the other side of the table where I could look down at his face.

Nguyen shook his head slowly. "No," he said, "I did not let him. It would not be a kindness to allow him to regain his strength now."

Nguyen's words made me realize that I was ashamed, not grateful, for my sleep. That annoyed me. Yet I could not deny that it seemed indecent for any of us to have slept through part of the boy's ordeal, even though it was Nguyen, and not the rest of us, who was tormenting him.

"What's he saying?" I asked.

"It is an old proverb," Nguyen answered evasively, and added that the boy had been talking like that most of the night, trying to finish a phrase that was beyond his reach. "I allow him to go on," he added, "since it does no harm to let him talk now. It may quicken his collapse."

The boy looked delirious. Nguyen went back to work on him, bending down and telling him to confess, and to sleep. The boy whispered as if he no longer heard anything that was said to him and was repeating some unknown sacrament in his own tongue. I thought that Nguyen was making a mistake by letting him go on. He was anesthetizing himself with his proverb, whatever it was, and no longer heard anything that

*121*

Nguyen said to him. But it was Nguyen's job, not mine, and I kept out of it. The boy's mouth was opening and closing with a regular pulse, like a fish. Now he was trying only to breathe, not to speak. His lips struggled for air and life. I lost control of my eyes when the thought of the prisoner's death again entered my mind. Freed for a moment, they strayed over his narrow chest to his groin. The flesh around the wounds was a variety of colors. It looked a little rotten.

"Has he said anything about the guerrillas?" I asked hopefully, forcing my eyes back to his face.

"No, he has said nothing but what you hear."

Nguyen was reluctant to speak to me, as if he did not trust me or because he did not want me to know. But I persisted, and finally he told me that mostly the boy was talking of his father and mother.

"He says they were killed a year ago in their village near Darlac."

"What else?" I asked.

Nguyen shrugged indifferently. "He also speaks of his sister, who is alone in Saigon, waiting for him."

"Then he's been telling the truth!" I said, glancing down at the boy's closed eyes.

Nguyen shook his head, and told me that I did not understand. "His parents were killed by American planes. He told me that he and his sister were in the rice fields working when the village was bombed. They saw everything, but they could not help. So you see," he said, looking at me with his eyes hidden in the shadow of the light, "he became a guerrilla."

"I wish I could be sure of that," I replied, feeling my eyes and face burning from the electric bulb that hung over us.

Nguyen studied me for a moment, while the sounds of the

boy's whisperings rose between us like the smoke of incense reaching upward to the light.

"Why does that matter to you?" he finally asked.

"Buckley won't stop until he has what he wants," I said, "and if the boy is innocent and has nothing to confess, Buckley will keep on until he kills him."

"Could he not have something to confess," Nguyen asked slowly, "and still be innocent?"

"That's none of my business," I said.

Nguyen watched me silently for a moment; then, warily, he asked me if I was ready to help him save the prisoner's life. "We do not have much time left," he added.

I did not like to hear him speak the actual words. It was as though he had brought something secret and ugly between us up into the light. Still, it was time. "I'm ready," I said, "if there's a way."

Nguyen bent toward me across the table, with the boy lying beneath us. "Only you and I understand the prisoner's words. They are nothing without us. If we help each other, there is a chance to save him." He spoke with an earnestness that I had never heard in his voice before, and which gave me an unpleasant sensation to hear now. But then he straightened up and added, "If you are on their side he will surely die, for then they have the language, and I am nothing."

"You have no reason to think that I'm on their side."

"You are an American," Nguyen replied.

"I'm a convict, under military sentence! Nothing more."

That seemed to satisfy him, and he relaxed. "I am grateful for your help," he said.

"I don't want your gratitude, but I'm willing to listen to you if you have a plan that will get us out of here."

He nodded, as if he understood exactly what I felt. "The boy is weak, and he is desperate," he said. "The information that he has held back for so long is rising to the top of his mind. He is afraid that he will give in to us."

"What then?"

Nguyen looked at me blankly, as if he did not understand. I had to repeat my question, and asked him what would happen if the boy confessed and told Buckley where the guerrillas were going to meet.

Nguyen shrugged and frowned, as though I had scattered his thoughts. "They will send him to a camp for rehabilitation of prisoners of war."

"But he'll live," I said, watching Nguyen's face closely.

"Of course," he said matter-of-factly. "Once they have their information they will forget him entirely. That is our only hope."

I wondered if he was right. Somehow I was certain that the boy would die, even if he confessed; but probably that was because I had faced a military court myself and did not trust the Army. A guerrilla, after all, was not as hated as a traitor.

"Do you think he'll talk?" I asked.

"If we are patient, yes, he will tell us everything."

I glanced at Buckley and McGruder, to see if they were awake.

"Do not worry about them now," Nguyen said quietly, following my eyes. "We must protect the prisoner from himself."

"What do you mean?"

"He has lost his fear of death. He wants only to escape. Twice during the night he reached for the knife—not to hurt me, for he knows that I am his friend—but to kill himself while he still has the strength left for it."

*124*

I looked down at the boy. His face was pale and sweating. He looked as though he was unconscious and in a high fever, but his lips were still moving. It was unnerving to watch, for no sound came out of his mouth—only empty breath, incapable of forming words any longer. When I looked up I saw Nguyen's hard eyes fixed upon me.

"All right," I said. "What do you want me to do?"

"We must be patient, and wait," he said. "With good luck we can keep him alive until his strength fails him. He is very weak. The end can't be far away for him now."

"There must be something we can do to make him talk before they wake up," I said, dreading the thought of it beginning again. There seemed no place left on the boy's body where he could be hurt without causing his death.

Nguyen looked at me strangely. "What would you suggest we do?" he asked. "You have seen how stubborn he is."

"I don't know!" I said, hating him for asking me that, as if I had been the one to use the knife. "But you know what will happen if McGruder gets his hands on him again. Warn the boy. Make him understand."

"It is you who do not understand," Nguyen replied. "McGruder is the prisoner's only hope now, for he knows that he will kill him. It is we, who want him to live by confessing, who are his enemies. I have told you that he is afraid of nothing except that he will betray his comrades."

I glanced involuntarily down at the knife, but Nguyen shook his head.

"No, not even the knife will help us now. He is too weak for it to have the proper effect. Sleeplessness and pressure will break him. Anything else will only kill him." He watched the boy's silently moving lips for a moment, as if he had learned to gauge the rise and fall of his strength by their slight movement, and then he looked up. "Sooner or later, if we do not lose patience, he will tell us everything."

"What do you want me to do?" I asked, already tired of my effort at conspiring with Nguyen, for we were caught with the prisoner and with each other, and our only hope lay in the boy's confession, or in his death.

"You are the lieutenant's friend," he said, without a trace of irony in his voice. "Keep him from losing patience. That is all I ask. I will do the rest."

"All right," I said, and agreed to do my part if a chance offered itself, since it seemed that we could not save ourselves without first saving the boy. Still, I was not sure that I could stop Buckley. If I tried, he would only become more suspicious, and therefore more dangerous. I glanced at the prisoner, feeling a little unhinged, for the words that Nguyen had used were unreal—they had no meaning when I tried to connect them with my idea of the boy. But then my idea of the boy was false. When I looked down at him I saw not a boy but a victim, badly wounded on the face and groin, who might quite reasonably want to die. Again his lips were forming inarticulate words. Then, when I looked up, gazing through the cone of painful light that fell across our eyes, I saw Buckley sitting on his cot, awake and watching us—and at that moment, without looking at the boy again, I caught the meaning of his words, which struck my ears like the sounds of a dead language suddenly remembered, for they were words of child-like supplication.

Now Russell and Finley were awake too. They were staring at us, like Buckley, only with fear rather than suspicion. Neither of them looked as though they had slept for a moment. The room was once again full of eyes. McGruder sat up, rubbed his unshaven jaw, and walked sullenly past Nguyen to the door. He went out, and a moment later we heard him urinating against the tin wall of the hut.

The sound seemed to arouse Buckley from his stupor and he rose with an effort and stood up. He circled the table, glaring from the prisoner to Nguyen, and then to me. There was a look of silent hatred in his swollen eyes, as if he had overheard every word that we had said. It struck me then that he had not slept at all, but that he had spent the long hours of the night leaning against the corrugated wall with his neck painfully bent, watching Nguyen and the boy out of half-closed eyelids. He was capable of it. He had the endurance of a maniac. I no longer thought of him as a man, but as something mechanical. Probably he had been watching me and straining to hear what I had said to Nguyen.

He turned the knife over and examined the dry edge. Then he raised his face under the light to peer accusingly at Nguyen. "Why hasn't it been used?" he asked, his voice thick with fatigue.

"He no longer feels it," Nguyen said, meeting his eyes without flinching.

Buckley's only answer was to jab the prisoner hard in the ribs with the dull point of the knife. The boy's mouth opened a little wider, but he showed no other sign of pain.

I felt cold all over. Nothing that Nguyen and I had said to one another would do any good. Suddenly I wanted to laugh. We had talked in the middle of the room like sleepwalkers, trying to awaken one another, and now the nightmare had begun again in spite of us. I looked at Buckley, hardly able to believe that I had seen him use the knife, for its use had unnerved him in the beginning as much as it had me. But after the night's vigil he seemed as benumbed as the prisoner, incapable of feeling anything. When I had first seen him, standing smoking next to the empty table the afternoon before, his face had been handsome; but now it was discolored and swollen. He looked in bad shape. Above all, he looked dangerous. Buckley held the power, and Nguyen and I, who had talked like fools, were helpless.

"All right, then we'll go on with it," Buckley said when he saw that the boy's face did not register the pain of the knife in his ribs. "See that he doesn't rest," he added, and threw the knife on the table.

I did not allow myself to look at Buckley, and now I avoided Nguyen's eyes too, for I did not want to be reminded that I was supposed to keep Buckley from losing his self-control. There was no way to do it. He was ready for anything now, and I wanted only to keep away from him. At the first attempt to placate him or to trick him he would seize the interrogation entirely and all that Nguyen and I had agreed upon would be lost in an instant. When I looked at Buckley's swollen and angry face I thought that I would be of more use to the boy if I remained in Buckley's confidence, where I would be able to influence him indirectly. Opposition would do no good. Persuasion was our only weapon, though, at the moment, he looked too dangerous for even that to be safe. More than ever I wanted to be alone, so I could recover my strength in some quiet and untroubled place where a man could forget that the room had ever existed. A feeling of cowardice came over me. It was a fear of moving, and seemed to be a part of the coldness of my body. It puzzled me, for I had never felt anything like it before; but then I realized that it was not for myself that I was afraid, but for the prisoner. If any of us made a false step it would be over in a flash of anger. We were all swollen with impatience now; and, like those condemned to the Plague, the price of the slightest movement would be death. It was the fate of the boy, not our honor, that mattered, and I tried to keep out of Buckley's way.

"You," Buckley said, turning angrily to Cowley, "go up to the mess and tell them to get our food and coffee in here, and to see that it's hot."

When I heard him say that, I remembered what Cowley had whispered to me about escaping. That had come to seem like a dream to me, but suddenly it was real. I forgot about the prisoner and Nguyen. "I'll go," I said, afraid that there would be trouble, and moved quickly in front of Cowley.

"Sit down!" Buckley shouted. "I'm still in command here. I'll give the orders." Then he turned to Cowley and said, "Get out of here and do what I told you."

Cowley scowled at me suspiciously and stood up. Buckley was exhausted and ill-tempered. I should have let Cowley go, but I knew that once he was allowed to get beyond the first barbed wire fence and the sentries outside the hut he would try to make it through the two that remained—and that he would get himself killed in the attempt. I made a quick decision, and told Buckley that Cowley was going to try to break out.

"You stinkin' bastard!" Cowley shouted, and lunged at me. But McGruder was on his feet and grabbed him from behind by both arms and held him back.

"What are you talking about?" Buckley demanded.

"He's going to try to escape the compound," I said. "He told me an hour ago, and asked me to go with him."

McGruder tightened his grip on Cowley to hold him still, but Cowley wasn't trying to move anymore; he was only standing with his hands open, staring at me as though he would begin to shout at the top of his lungs, or begin to cry.

"What about it?" Buckley asked, moving toward him with an angry look in his eyes.

Cowley refused to say anything. It was left to me to explain to Buckley that he wanted to get away from the room so badly that he was willing to risk his life by trying to escape from the camp.

"We know how to take care of this guy," McGruder said, and began to shove Cowley toward the door. I thought that Cowley would fight, for he had gone at McGruder with a hammer the night before, but now he did not. All of his anger had been drained out of him, and he was lifeless and dull in McGruder's grasp.

"What's your part in this, Kreuger?" Buckley asked, turning his distrustful gaze toward me.

"Only what I've told you. I tried to talk him out of it, but he wouldn't listen."

"You bastard," Cowley whispered.

"Keep your mouth shut," McGruder grunted and jerked Cowley's arms back until his head was pushed forward. Then he looked up at Buckley. "I'll take him to the stockade. They'll fix him so he won't go anywhere for a long time."

"No," I said. "He'll talk in the stockade, no matter where they put him. The whole camp will know what's going on inside here."

"What'll we do with him?" McGruder asked.

"Leave him alone," I said.

Buckley nodded, and agreed. Cowley was watching me,

his chest rising and falling with hard breathing. No doubt he would have killed me if we had been outside. But here, inside, he was whipped. I didn't care what he thought. He had been lucky and was too stupid to realize it. So had the rest of us. If he had broken out, taking what he knew with him, Buckley would have finished the boy on the spot. Now Cowley would live, instead of being shot at the fences, and the room itself had become a little safer. Buckley was regarding me with an expression that was almost one of confidence. A short time before he had thought that I was Nguyen's accomplice. Now I had handed Cowley over to him. My influence with him had grown. None of them understood that I had done it to save the prisoner, but Buckley looked more reasonable and that was all that mattered to me. I knew, at last, how to deal with him.

"You get the food from the mess," Buckley said to me, jerking his head toward the door and glancing down at the prisoner.

"What's to keep him from going over the wall, too?" McGruder demanded, angry at having lost the chance of getting Cowley alone inside the stockade for punishment. Now he wanted me. "Send Russell," he said.

"No," Buckley replied evasively, "I'm going to need Russell."

McGruder watched me belligerently, still holding Cowley from behind, as if he thought that I was about to escape for good. "He's a jailbird, just the same as this one," he said sullenly.

Buckley glanced up at me, and a half smile, unpleasant to see on his swollen and humorless face, appeared at the corners of his mouth. "Kreuger will come back," he said, "because he's smart enough to know he has no choice."

Still McGruder was stubborn, and said that it was no good letting me go alone. "He can't walk through the camp dressed like that," he muttered.

Buckley became irritated and told him to shut up, but he turned to the door and called one of the sentries. He seemed eager to have me out of the room under any circumstances— by myself or at gun point didn't matter. "Take him to the mess and bring him back," he said, pointing to me; and then he glanced back at me with a look of tacit understanding in his eyes, as if he thought that I had stopped Cowley for our benefit alone.

The sentry motioned wordlessly for me to follow him. I left the hut without saying anything, wanting to do whatever would avoid trouble. But as soon as I stepped outside the door an uncontrollable sense of liberation came over me. The sky was already a gentle gray, and the sounds of muted voices and of cold engines was on the morning air. Within thirty minutes the sun would rise above the seaward horizon, as peacefully as I had seen it rise the day before. The air was soft and cool on my skin, and I walked away from the hut and the sleepy sentry who remained by the opening in the fence, letting it soothe my burning face. We went through the motor pool, where rows of trucks with the dew of night mists still on their windshields were lined up facing the beach, waiting for the sun with blind eyes.

I didn't look back. After we had gone a hundred yards it was difficult to believe that the inside of the room actually existed, or that any of the men left in it were more than a nightmare. Everything in the outer world looked peaceful and normal. It seemed limitless. I wondered if I had dreamed it all because of the fever that Mason's serum had put into me. The thought so relieved me that I almost laughed out loud; but the laugh was going to be hysterical, and I kept it back and walked on, trying not to lose control of myself just when I had escaped the hut. From the place where we came through the first fence I could see the two fences that remained, and, like Cowley, I wanted badly to get over them. The only difference was that, unlike Cowley, I knew that it was useless to try. We would have to save ourselves in some other way.

I tried to talk to the guard, if only to hear the sound of a voice that was innocent of what was happening in the shed. "It's going to be hot," I said.

He peered up at the cloudless sky. "Yeah," he said, and then he brought his eyes back to me as if I had tricked him. His look of distrust made me feel the futility of talking to him, but I tried nevertheless and said that he would have tough duty if he had to stay outside the hut.

"You just keep walking," he answered, and slipped his right hand down the stock of his rifle toward the trigger.

There were small figures of convicts working in the sand. I longed to turn toward the beach and rejoin them. There were guards that I recognized by the gate. They were tough, but you knew what to expect from them and how to keep out of trouble when they came around. I saw a man who could have been Smith, or the new kid who had been in such bad shape the day before. It was hard to tell for sure who they were, they were so far away. A jeep's engine started up behind a nearby barracks, and I saw two soldiers with sunglasses and soft fatigue hats drive toward the main gate. There were towels and swimming trunks in the back seat. They went through the gate without stopping and turned at a leisurely speed toward the southern end of the bay, away from Quai

Dong, as if they had all day. I watched them as long as I could, but I stumbled and nearly fell and the guard told me to look where I was going.

We crossed the parade ground and went around the rows of tents behind the command post to the mess. Inside there were clean wooden tables and metal chairs. The aroma of strong coffee was on the air, hot, and the smell of frying bacon. I thought for a second of the rotten food that we had in the stockade. Already, even in the room with the prisoner, I was eating better than I had. The guard told me to stop in the center of the mess hall, and then he called out. We waited. In a minute a cook in a clean white apron and a tall hat came toward us, squinting at my dirty stockade uniform and at the guard behind me.

"What's this?" he asked.

I told him that Lieutenant Buckley wanted coffee and breakfast in the maintenance shed.

"Okay," he said, "we'll send it. It was coming anyway."

"I'll take it back with me," I said.

He shrugged and said that it was all the same to him, since it would save time for them if I did; but he peered at me strangely, as if wondering what I was doing outside the stockade. "You people have one of our cans down there now," he said. "I sent five last night, and you only put four back where we could get them."

"I'll look for it," I said.

"It's no joke, you know. We got seven hundred men to feed, and nothing to do it with as it is."

I promised to give him back the can, and he went back through two swinging doors and left us alone. There seemed no reason to stand, so I sat down on a chair. The guard stood awkwardly over me, but he didn't tell me to stand up. Then, after a minute, he let his rifle rest on the floor between his knees and sat down too.

The mess was warm from the heat of stoves and open ovens. On top of the coffee and meat there was a rich smell of hot bread. I began to feel my hunger for the first time since they had taken me out of the stockade lineup the afternoon before. For a moment I heard voices outside and thought that officers were coming in; I hated that, because then I would have to stand up. The standing didn't bother me, but I didn't want to have them staring at me. I was ashamed of my ragged clothes and of my stubble of beard. I felt suddenly like a criminal, and ran my fingers through my hair to straighten it as much as I could, though none of us had ever thought of it that way in the stockade.

But the voices passed by and we were left alone. I let my face rest in my hands and gazed at the floor between my feet. Soon I began to doze. My mind wandered, numbly, and the heat of the room made my face throb pleasantly. When a noise aroused me I tried to sink back.

Twenty minutes passed before they brought the food out to us. It was packed in aluminum canisters, and it was hot. I had to get up then, but some of the food was for me and I didn't mind so much. There was more than I could carry alone. The guard looked at the cans uneasily, but when I asked him to help me he slung his rifle over his shoulder without arguing and let the cook pile half the cans in his arms. We left together and headed back across the parade ground.

Outside, the first pink rays of the sun were striking across the tops of barrack walls. The open sky overhead had turned from gray to a tranquil morning blue, with something indefinably golden in it. A strange sensation of happiness came over me, and I looked at the guard. "You're in B company," I said, noticing his arm patch.

"Yeah," he answered. "I was supposed to be on Guam."

"How long have you been out here?"

"Three months. I got nine months, two weeks, and four days of it left, the way I figure, and then they have to send me home."

He grinned at me, and I nodded, thinking that he was lucky. I had almost forgotten what my home was like, my hope of ever seeing it again had fallen so low. I didn't want to think about it and asked him what his name was.

"Jackson," he replied.

"Where you from?" I asked.

"Oregon," he said. "A little crossroad town outside Salem. A very nice place. You?"

"Oh, not far from Cleveland."

"On a farm?"

"Not exactly."

"You married?" he asked.

"No," I said.

He half laughed, half grunted. "I'm supposed to have a girl waiting for me," he said, "but I don't believe it."

We went on in silence for a moment, then he squinted up at me. "What'd you ever do to get put in that stockade, anyway?"

"I refused an order," I said. He let it alone and seemed to be thinking. Here and there other groups of men were coming slowly out of the round-roofed huts, stretching and heading for their breakfast, but now I did not feel conspicuous. No-

*136*

body paid any attention to us. We looked like two ordinary G.I.'s walking side by side with our arms full of cans.

Finally Jackson began to talk again. "What are you guys doing in that shed?" he asked, and I realized that he dreaded it too, for reasons of his own.

I didn't say anything, for nothing came to my mind quickly enough.

But he went on as if he didn't care. "You have it easy inside," he complained. "We're gonna rot in that lousy sun today."

I said that he was right, and I almost felt sorry for him. We passed through the fence around the maintenance yard and I found, to my surprise, that I did not want to escape over it so badly now that the guard was walking beside me, instead of behind me. I did not feel like a convict, nor so hopeless, when the muzzle of his gun was not pointed at my back. He felt it too, and was talkative, as if he were relieved of his fear of me when he did not have to watch my every move.

But when we turned around the row of trucks and saw the squat box of the hut the terror returned to both of us. Ragged coils of barbed wire surrounded the low walls. The guards were now posted at three corners of the fence. The tin door was tightly shut. It looked as if it had been nailed in, like a coffin lid, without a hole for a man to breathe through and with a broken ceiling so low you could barely stand up.

The guard was silent. He wanted to shift the cans to one arm so that he could reach back for his gun. I felt it too. My place was in front of him, and all my hatred for him came back. We neared the gap in the barbed wire in silence, and then he suddenly shoved the cans that he had carried on top

*137*

of those in my arms and left me to rejoin the other guards, who had watched us approach without a word or a sign. I realized that I had been a fool to come back so soon, but I had forgotten, in my moment of freedom, what the room did to a man. Now it was too late.

CHAPTER *SIX*

"SHUT THE DOOR!" Buckley screamed when I entered the room.

At first my eyes were blinded from the bright morning light outside. I couldn't see anything, for the inside of the hut seemed to be completely dark. But then the electric light grew steadily brighter until it burned my eyes like an open flame, and I saw the room, exactly as I had left it.

The only difference now was that Buckley himself was standing under the electric bulb. He was facing the table and the motionless figure of the boy, with the light illuminating the tips of his ears and the back of his neck; and when he turned to shout his warning at me it fell across his face like a white mask. It was still the middle of the night inside the hut.

The boy had been pulled into a sitting position on the table, where his legs hung over the edge. Russell supported him from behind. The long black hands reluctantly gripped the pale yellow shoulders, but it was Buckley's hands that I watched. They were opening and closing with impotent fury. At first I didn't understand what had enraged him so, but then I heard the weak whispering of the prisoner's voice. He was gasping out inarticulate sounds. Now and then his legs twitched as if he were unable to bear their immobility any longer, and I saw that he had urinated on the floor.

"What's he saying?" Buckley demanded, looking at me

*141*

but still listening fixedly to the short rasping sounds that came up from the boy's throat, almost unformed by his stiffened lips, like an enfeebled wind that carried the faded sound of a far-off voice.

I put the cans down on the floor under my cot and tried to piece together what he was trying to say, but I couldn't make it out. I looked quickly at Nguyen to see what he wanted me to do.

"No," Buckley warned, "I want it from you."

I tried to think clearly, but he gave me no time. "He's asking you to let him rest," I said.

Probably my guess was right, but it wasn't enough to satisfy Buckley. Nothing would satisfy him but what he wanted to hear—the confession, and the name of the village or rice field where the guerrillas hid their arms. He picked up the knife and turned the point of it toward Nguyen.

"What did the boy say to me?" he asked, edging around the table with the handle of the knife balanced in the open palm of his hand as if he were offering the knife as a reward, or threatening to grip it suddenly and attack him with it.

For a second Nguyen looked at me; then, when Buckley was close enough to reach him, he stepped quickly back. "He has said nothing of importance," he answered quietly, but he kept his eyes on the knife.

"Answer me," Buckley said, "or I'll use this!"

With a sudden snap he closed his fingers around the handle of the knife and jerked it upward in an evil slice, making the blade flash in the light. Nguyen kept away from him. They stared at each other for a moment, and then Nguyen lowered his eyes.

"The prisoner is calling for his family to help him," he

said. "He is Buddhist and he thinks that you will kill him now. His ancestors are sacred to him."

Buckley turned away. He should have been pleased, for we had been inept and he had easily trapped us—but instead he began to swear, not loudly, but viciously. He could not trust either of us now, and his hope of breaking the boy was therefore farther from his reach than ever. He stood by himself for a moment; then he looked up and told Nguyen to get away from the table.

"I'll interrogate the prisoner myself," he said.

Nguyen remained stubbornly under the light and would not move. For a moment I thought that he would defy Buckley, who held the knife, and I moved out of the way.

"You must let me do it," Nguyen said.

Buckley lowered his head ominously. "I'll put you under arrest if you don't stand aside," he said quietly.

Suddenly, without warning, Nguyen drew himself up and cried, "I am a Vietnamese!"

His shout startled all of us. There had been no outward sign of his anger, but when he had tried to speak only a shrill cry of hate had come out.

"As long as you're at Quai Dong you'll do what we tell you," Buckley answered.

"Please give me the knife," Nguyen said, controlling himself with an immense effort.

Buckley signaled to McGruder and moved slowly forward. "I'll give you ten seconds," he said, "to get away from the table."

"I am his interrogator!" Nguyen shrieked.

"You're nothing but what I say you are," Buckley replied. "I'll interrogate him now. You're finished."

At that Nguyen lunged for the door. It was the lack of sleep, and his hatred for Buckley. But then he turned around abruptly, as if remembering that I was in the room. He controlled himself and sat down on an empty cot with a look of sudden and complete exhaustion masking his face.

I was ashamed of him. Like all Orientals, he shrieked when he was angry. Buckley, at least, was a man. Now McGruder was waiting next to the far side of the table, as if his time had come. His eyes moved quickly from Buckley to Nguyen and then back to the knife.

"Lieutenant?" he said expectantly.

His voice irritated Buckley. "Sit down!" he shouted; and then he added, in a quieter tone, "I'm only going to question him."

Nguyen glanced at me, and I stood up uneasily and told Buckley that I would translate for him. More than anything else, it was the way that he held the knife that made me want to place myself between him and the boy.

But he told me to keep away. "I don't need you for this," he said. "He knows well enough what I want out of him."

No doubt he was right. There seemed nothing for me to do. I looked back at Nguyen, but he kept his eyes fixed sullenly on the knife and paid no attention to me, though I had stood up at his bidding. Buckley held the knife awkwardly beneath the table, as if he were hiding it from the boy. He bent over him and ordered him to tell him where he had been instructed to meet the guerrillas. "I'm not going to hurt you," he said, and he repeated his demand for confession over and over, as though he did not understand that the boy would never answer.

I stayed near the table, watching the little jerks that the

knife was making in Buckley's stiff hand. I knew that I would
have to stop him if he tried to use it on the boy. Unlike
Nguyen, he could not be trusted to keep himself from plung-
ing the entire blade into the boy's stomach. He would kill
him. There would be a fight. With McGruder in the room,
and with Cowley now indifferent to our fate, we would not
have a chance. The guards would rush in and it would end
with our arrests. The interrogation would go on without us,
and in that case the boy would die as surely as if Buckley
were allowed to use the knife unhindered now. There was
nothing to do, in either case; nor would the prisoner help us.
He refused to utter a sound, and provoked Buckley by staring
up at him with his jaw set firmly shut.

"Get away," Buckley warned when he saw me watching
him, and he kept his eyes on me until I had returned to my
cot, as though he did not want me to see the boy resisting
him, or because he distrusted me now as much as Nguyen.
Only when I sat against the wall did he return to the boy and
repeat his useless demand for confession.

By ten o'clock Buckley's voice had risen to a high and
ineffectual complaint. He was tormenting himself and growing more desperately impatient with every minute that
passed.

Nguyen moved uneasily next to me. "He will use the
knife!" he whispered.

"No," I said, "he doesn't dare to kill him, not until he
talks."

Nguyen clenched his fists. "I have done everything that
I can," he said, "but now it is over."

For a second the thought passed through my mind that
if Nguyen were right, I would be allowed to go back to the

*145*

mindless work on the beach; for, with the boy dead, we would all be set free. But Nguyen slumped forward with his elbows on his knees, giving in at last to his fatigue. He looked so hopeless that I recovered my thoughts and tried to think of some way of intervening between Buckley and the prisoner.

Finley and Russell had come silently toward us when McGruder moved to the other side of the table to be near Buckley. Now we four were sitting together like sheep huddled for protection on the two cots, watching the boy and the knife with growing apprehension. When I tried to consider the prisoner my mind was a blank. Then I remembered the cans of food under my cot. I opened them, feeling their comforting heat on my hands, and let the aroma of hot coffee and bacon fill the room.

The others would not eat, but I took my share of the food and forced myself to swallow it. I had no appetite, but I ate what I could, since it seemed necessary to keep up my strength. My stomach was almost too tight to accept the food, with Buckley shouting menacingly at the boy, but I reminded myself that we might be in the room for days yet; and I found, among other things, that one could eat as well as sleep in the presence of the boy and the knife. McGruder took six cans and filled his mouth with great spoonfuls of cereal which he washed down with coffee. I felt sorry for Cowley and tried to make him eat. He refused, and sat on the ground with his head against the wall, his face sunken, as if he had no more life in him, watching Buckley and the prisoner without a sound.

Russell couldn't watch me eating, and turned away toward Nguyen.

*146*

"How old is he?" he whispered, looking up into the light.

"Who?" Nguyen asked, raising his head wearily.

Russell nodded toward the prisoner. "When I looked at his face . . . before I got sick," he said, "I couldn't tell how old he was." He closed his eyes tightly, as though remembering a nightmare, and added, "He looked so old, that I'd never seen anything like it before."

"He's eighteen," Nguyen said indifferently, lowering his head again until it rested in his arms, "nineteen at most."

"But man, his face!"

"He was in pain," Nguyen murmured.

Russell shook his head slowly, as if unable to believe it; then he whispered, "I don't see how you could do that to him. He's one of your own people."

"Shut up," I said.

But Nguyen looked up at Russell without anger. "Have you killed a man yet?" he asked.

Russell shook his head vehemently. "No *sir*."

"Then you do not know enough to ask me such a question. In my village every man over sixteen was shot by the Viet Cong. We have seen death."

Russell left him alone then. Nguyen was no more intelligible to me than before, but he looked suddenly more human. The light that I had seen in his eyes when he had asked me to help him was dead now. He was finished, burned out, and seemed, like Cowley, to have washed his hands of the entire affair. For a moment I regretted that I had not stood firmly by him at the first chance, instead of waiting. But it was too late now, in any case. One could not choose between survival and torture without first seeing how bad the torture

147

could be. None of us had known, except maybe Nguyen. Only now did the rest of us understand what it was like, and how little effect it had, and that it had to be stopped.

"Listen!" Finley said, grabbing my arm, for the prisoner had suddenly cried out. Nguyen jumped instantly to his feet, certain that Buckley had lost his patience and stabbed him. But the knife was still in his hand, out of sight in the slanting shadow beneath the table. The boy's head was raised stiffly off the metal surface, his thin neck muscles straining. He was staring directly at Buckley. The swollen lips were drawn apart and the teeth were exposed in such a grimace of hate that even Buckley had taken an involuntary step backwards.

"What is it?" he asked when he saw Nguyen standing next to him.

Nguyen listened to the boy's shrill words; then he moved away and would not look at Buckley again.

I heard it too. My face felt suddenly hot. I thought that I would break into a laugh, but the boy's voice was so shrill that I feared the sound of laughter and controlled myself.

The prisoner was too weak to shout. Instead, he had shrieked like a girl. Then his strength failed him completely and he sank back, gasping, but still staring up at Buckley's face.

"It is of no importance," Nguyen replied when Buckley asked him again what the boy had tried to say.

Buckley brought the knife up under Nguyen's chin and warned him to repeat the prisoner's words exactly. "Don't change a word," he whispered, and tightened the muscles of his forearm until it seemed that the knife would go through Nguyen's throat.

"The prisoner said that he despises you," Nguyen replied, looking at Buckley with a completely indifferent face.

At first Buckley's expression was blank, and then he became impatient; but he did not seem angry. "He said more than that," he insisted, but he lowered the knife as if he knew that he would get nothing more from Nguyen.

Nguyen shrugged. "That is the only way I can translate it," he said.

"Kreuger!" Buckley shouted, turning around and looking hopefully at me.

Again he had placed himself in our hands, asking for the help that we alone could give. I looked at Nguyen, but he made no sign to me and seemed not to care or not to see that we might help each other if we were quick. For a moment I tried to think of something to say that would save us, while Buckley waited with a look of growing distrust. But everything seemed too dangerous, and I simply agreed with Nguyen. "That's all that the boy said," I told him.

Then Buckley was furious, both at us and at the prisoner, and he turned despairingly back to the boy and rose over him as if he would use the knife.

"You see," Nguyen said calmly, "he wants you to kill him. He is trying to trick you."

Buckley restrained himself. His head and neck went stiff for a moment, but he had reserves that I had not yet seen, and he put the knife quietly on the table. He remained with his back to us for a moment longer, staring down at the prisoner; then he turned around, his face perfectly composed, and told Nguyen to pick up the knife.

"Go back to work, Sergeant," he said. "Put him on his feet. Use the knife on his stomach."

Nguyen took the knife eagerly, balancing it in his hand as if grateful to feel it in his possession again, but he hesitated. "It will be best not to use it anymore," he said, speaking cautiously and watching Buckley out of the corner of his eye.

Buckley, however, had not surrendered his authority—only the knife. He ordered Nguyen to work the groin again, exactly where he had before, and then he stepped out of the light and motioned McGruder back, leaving Nguyen entirely alone with the boy, as he had been in the beginning.

Nguyen did not dare to argue. There was nothing to do but raise the boy into a sitting position on the edge of the table and then force him to stand on the floor. Buckley made Russell and Finley help him. They went reluctantly, but the three of them finally pulled the boy to his feet. He seemed to have no life remaining in his legs. Now Buckley was patient, however, and he watched without interfering while Nguyen massaged the boy's thighs and calves until he could stand, supported by Russell and Finley. Buckley was satisfied when they were finished, and sat down next to me. He kept his eyes on them, bending forward into the cone of light that fell from the ceiling until he was sure that his order was being carried out. Nguyen went to work with a sudden attack on the boy. Then Buckley turned to me with such a look of secret complicity in his eyes that I was afraid that he would try to put his hand on my shoulder again.

"Let's get this thing straight between the two of us," he said quietly, gazing at me with a steady look, and moving close to me. "Nguyen has been lying to us from the beginning. The boy must have told him something in all this time."

Buckley made me sick. I shook my head and told him that he was mistaken, but he was incapable of understanding.

"You've been lying to me, too," he added, with a soft tone of menace in his voice that reminded me of my stockade uniform. "I'm not going to come down on you for that because I'm only interested in information. But it has to stop, now. I've been very patient with you."

I told him that I didn't know what the boy might have told Nguyen during the night, but that if he told him anything I hadn't heard it. "I slept," I said.

Buckley seemed encouraged, and moved closer. "Listen to me, Kreuger. You hate the sight of me. All right, to me you're a stinking convict that isn't worth a bullet. But we don't have any choice now that we're in this together but to help each other. It's the only way out for either of us. I'm willing to trust you because I don't have anyone else. You'll have to help me for the same reason, or you'll never come through this." He watched me in silence for a moment, studying my face hopefully; then, in a voice that contained all the suppressed vexation of the long hours of questioning, he added, "I know that the boy has told Nguyen everything!"

I remained silent, watching Nguyen once again using the knife with his deadly short jabs, and I felt it each time as if my own body was as bruised and unable to bear the pain of the steel as the boy's.

Buckley looked up at them too, and began to plead with me. "Tell me what you know, Kreuger. For the love of God, tell me so I can put a stop to this," he said. "I'm not asking for myself anymore. It's the boy who's suffering now."

His words, spoken in so low a voice that only I could hear them, had such a false sound in them that my preoccupation with the unnerving thrusts of the knife was broken. I peered directly into Buckley's haggard face. There was something

**151**

moving in his eyes that was demented and pleading and yet treacherous. The desire to fight him was strong in me; but the boy would pay for it, and so would the rest of us. After all, he had the power, and we had nothing. I resisted the opportunity that his eagerness had placed within my reach, though it would have been so easy to deceive him.

"I'd tell you if I knew anything. Why should I lie to you?" I asked, forcing myself to look back into the light, where the point of the knife made glinting arcs as Nguyen swung it steadily from the level of his thigh up to the boy's bleeding stomach, drew it back, and swung it again. "As far as I know," I said, "the prisoner hasn't told Nguyen a thing."

Buckley leaned back. He closed his eyes and began to swear. I continued to watch the knife, which was doing its work with the precision and regularity of a pendulum. Nguyen was more than carrying out Buckley's orders. He seemed to have changed his mind about the utility of the knife and was making one last try at breaking the boy's resistance before McGruder took his place again. Thus he gave in to necessity, hoping for the best; but the prisoner was too weak to stand much of it now. The old wounds, which had formed thinly drawn scabs, were being reopened, one by one. Nguyen screamed at the top of his voice for confession, but the boy's only response was to screw his face into a motionless expression of pain and to roll his head violently from side to side in rhythm with the swing of the knife that punctured his flesh. Finley's and Russell's faces were bloodless and stiff. They tried to keep their eyes off the knife, but of course they could feel the boy's body jerk spasmodically every time Nguyen struck. Quietly, in some yet-untroubled part of my mind, I noted that they too, in their desire to help the boy, had become unwitting accomplices to his torture.

"You've got to help me," Buckley said, pulling himself up and beginning again, as if, in his brief moment of rest, he had thought the whole matter through from beginning to end. He seemed confident, and was not so much asking me to help him as expressing aloud the conviction that it was inevitable that I must.

"You have the major's word for it that there's a full reinstatement waiting for you when we leave this room with the information that he needs," he said. And then he added, as if to reassure himself, "No man would pass that up."

Each time that Buckley said that to me I wanted to cover my face, or hit him with my fists. But my face was thick and heavy, and my insides felt too rotten to move.

"The boy said exactly what Nguyen told you," I answered quietly. "Most of all," I said, looking at his swollen face, "he despises you."

"Yes, but he said more than that," Buckley insisted, frowning with disbelief.

My anger collapsed in the face of his stupidity. My head began to ache. "The language is like that," I said, wanting only to be left alone so that I could sit with Cowley in a far corner and wait for events to free us by taking their natural course.

Buckley slipped his fingers around my arm as if to urge me further, and began to repeat the major's exact words to me, when suddenly there was a loud clang of metal. Both of us jumped off the cot, thinking that something had been thrown at us.

"It is no good to use the groin!" Nguyen shouted, beside himself with rage. "You see that he cannot stand it! This is not the proper way!"

He had thrown the knife down on the table, for the boy had fainted. He had tumbled to the left, toward Russell, who was holding him around the middle with his hands on the slippery wounds on his stomach. With a great effort he was trying to lift him back onto the table, but Finley would not help him, and Russell looked like he was going to faint himself.

"Drop him on the floor," Buckley said, and Russell let go.

The boy fell with his head and shoulders under the table, out of the light. Russell held his bloodstained hands out in front of him and begged to be allowed to leave the room. I noticed, with the strange lucidity of exhaustion, that it was only on the upturned palms of his hands, where the skin was white, that one could see the blood. Buckley ignored him and told Finley to examine the prisoner. Russell's face was covered with tears. I thought that he was beginning to weep. I stood up, hating to see it, and took him by the arm and made him come to my cot and sit down. The bucket was empty. We had no water left, so I poured cold coffee over his hands.

"Wipe them," I said.

He was shaking too hard to be able to help himself. I wrapped his hands in a cloth and forced them between his knees. In a minute he rolled over on his side like a child, staring at the wall with tears running across his face. He was not blinking, but he seemed all right and I left him alone.

Finley was not able to revive the prisoner. He had given him the usual shot, but this time nothing happened. When Nguyen dragged the boy back into the light we could see that his pulse was beating faintly in his neck. He was not dead.

Buckley told Finley to keep giving him the injections until he came around.

"It might kill him," Finley whispered.

"Damn it, do what I tell you!" Buckley cried, beside himself now that even Finley was ready to argue with him. "I'm in command here. Do I have to prove it to you?"

Finley was silent and gave the boy two more shots, and waited, shaking his head. I suppose that he thought he had killed him. Nguyen stood over them, outwardly calm after his outburst. The knife had slid hard across the table when he threw it down, and it had fallen in the dirt on the far side at McGruder's feet. Nguyen made no effort to recover it. He seemed no longer to want it.

The third shot took effect, and the boy's eyes slowly opened. He blinked in the light. Finley took his pulse. He looked up, with a white face, and said that it was a hundred and forty.

"Stand him on his feet," Buckley answered.

Finley raised him up slowly, but when he let him go the boy fell back in a heap on the floor.

"Again," Buckley said. "He's faking."

Once more Finley pulled him up, and again he fell back. His legs would not hold him. Buckley ordered Finley to do it a third and a fourth time, but when he told him to lift the boy for the fifth time Finley remained on his hands and knees beside the body of the prisoner, his head down, and did not move. Buckley repeated his order in a calm voice, but Finley seemed no longer able to hear, and would not look up.

Buckley showed no sign of anger. He simply put his hands in his pockets and said, "All right," and then he told

McGruder—he called him "Sergeant McGruder" now—to stand the prisoner up so the interrogation could go on.

The moment that we had learned to dread most had finally come. I had opposed Buckley to the limit of my power. Now I felt my impotence. Neither Finley nor Cowley could do anything to interfere. But before McGruder could lay his hands on the boy Nguyen stepped forward. He raised him and stood beside him with his arm around his waist to keep him from falling. Neither of them made a sound. The boy's head and arms hung limply against Nguyen's chest, but he was on his feet.

Buckley gazed at them for a moment. "That's very good of you, Sergeant, but it's too late," he said, as though he had finally trapped the two Vietnamese together and was pleased. He motioned to McGruder, who moved past me and shoved Nguyen to one side. Nguyen stumbled, for he was tired, but he managed to keep his feet.

And then, once more, as if nothing had come out of all our effort in the intervening hours, I saw McGruder take the boy by the throat and put his fist in front of his face, raising the blow that would put an end to everything—but before he brought his fist down the boy opened his swollen lips and cried out. The unexpected sound startled even McGruder so much that he let the boy go, and he slumped against the table but did not fall. Buckley leaped forward, listening intensely and peering eagerly at the boy's twisted face, which was still swollen and stiff with blood from the grip of McGruder's fingers around his thin throat.

"What did he say?" Buckley whispered, looking at all of us in turn, even at Russell and Cowley, as if he had gone mad and thought that they too could tell him all that he wanted to know.

Nguyen refused to say anything.

"Kreuger, for Christ's sake," Buckley shouted, "this is our last chance! What did the kid say?"

It was left for me to tell him that it was only another cry of hate, and now of defiance as well. Buckley stared at me with a look of wild distrust, as though he was afraid to believe me. McGruder was looking at all of us, even at Buckley, thinking that we were finished.

The boy continued to utter his weak but persistent cry. He had revived enough to support himself against the edge of the table with his hands. Though he could not hold his head up, he continued to make his hoarse sounds of defiance. His body was half the size of McGruder's, yet he was standing less than a foot from him, nearly unconscious, and fighting us all with a diabolical pleasure in seeing us defeated. His voice frightened me, for I did not think that he would be so reckless unless he felt himself near death and had nothing more to fear from any of us. I wanted to hit him to make him shut up.

Buckley was frantic. He walked around the table, insisting that the sight of McGruder's fist had frightened the boy into confession. "You're a bunch of murderous bastards!" he shouted. "You want this to happen! Why won't any of you tell me the truth?"

There was no answer. Finally Buckley grabbed the edge of the table with his hands and glared at Nguyen and at me; then, with a twitch at the corner of his mouth, he turned his head toward McGruder. "Go ahead," he said.

*157*

Still the room was deathly silent, except for the exhausted whisperings of the boy. Buckley looked back at us, his eyes gleaming, waiting, but met only our silent faces—and then he ordered McGruder to stop.

"Do you want to see him killed?" he asked, unable to believe that we could not help him.

He seemed amazed, and for the first time I saw that he was as frightened of McGruder as we were. Even more than the rest of us, he wanted the prisoner alive for whatever it was that he had been sent to get out of him.

Many thoughts lay scattered through my mind. Facing Buckley, with McGruder waiting under the light, I wanted desperately to do something; but I knew that nothing would be of any good to us now. There was nothing to say to Buckley, for the prisoner had not confessed. I waited, forcing myself to remain detached; and then, at last, Buckley lost control of himself, as I knew he would, and he signaled savagely to McGruder, who instantly struck the prisoner's head with his doubled fist. This time he struck hard. It was over in a second. The boy was knocked across the room and fell on his face. Nothing moved. My overstrained nerves sagged with an immense relief, for now it was finished. We had nothing more to fear. I felt strangely at peace, as if, after a long and uncertain descent, I lay finally settled on the soft bottom of a motionless sea, looking up through clear depths to the troubled surface where the small images of men continued to struggle. But now they moved with dreamlike slowness, with no terror left in them, for the boy had escaped. Then the room, frozen for so long, seemed to move. There was a vicious sound behind me. I could hear my own breathing and the pounding of my own heart; and suddenly I realized that the boy was surely dead, and that everything was finished, and that it had ended in murder, and that I had done nothing to prevent it. I knew then that I was going to attack McGruder, and I turned slowly, feeling as though I had gone mad—but saw that Nguyen had already thrown himself at him and had been slapped so violently across the face that he was leaning over the table, dazed and bleeding.

The sound of that slap, like a rock hitting wet meat, drew me back to the surface of things, where I stood chilled, but with clear vision. I looked around the room—the prisoner was lying crumpled in a corner; Finley had scrambled to his feet and was standing over his medical pack; Russell was lying on the cot, gazing at the wall, as though he saw nothing; Cowley's face was white and stiff in the hard light, yet he remained on the floor as though he no longer feared anything for himself; and Nguyen was slowly pulling himself up, with his mouth and right eye bleeding, while Buckley and McGruder and I looked at one another as though nothing had happened.

Buckley was the first to move. He opened the door and ordered two sentries into the room. Then he turned to Nguyen: "You're under military arrest," he said.

Sunlight burst into the room from the opened doorway, and in its sudden brilliance my eyes were drawn away from Nguyen. I looked out of the hut. I could see the barbed wire and the camp beyond it clearly. Everything was golden outside. A square of sunlight fell across the floor and reached halfway up the legs of the table, in spite of the efforts of the electric bulb to diminish it. Somewhere behind me the guards were searching Nguyen. He did not resist. In that light of the real world nothing that had taken place inside the closed room held any importance, even to me. When Nguyen was led past I saw that the blood from his eyes had reached his neck, where it was lost in the shadow under his jaw.

"Take him to the stockade and put him under maximum detention until we can get hold of someone from Saigon to pick him up," Buckley said, and Nguyen left the room between two guards without looking at any of us and without uttering another word. The door was closed; and only then, when the sharp turn of the lock echoed against the walls and shut out the daylight, did I realize that I was left entirely alone.

"Put the prisoner on the table," Buckley said. "We're going to finish this now."

McGruder lifted the boy effortlessly and dropped him on the metal table as though he were a rag doll. Finley was forced to examine him. He was too worn out to do anything for him, but he pulled his eyelids open and tried to find his pulse.

"I think he's dying," he whispered.

Buckley peered over his shoulder and looked irritably down at the boy. "It's your job to keep him alive," he snapped.

Finley shook his head and closed his eyes, as if he couldn't stand anymore. He said that the prisoner was in shock. "Cover him with blankets. That's all I know."

The blankets were hurriedly pulled off the cots and laid over the boy's body. They hid the wounds on the stomach and back. All that we could see was his face, with the blanket tucked across his chest; but the face was lifeless.

Buckley was angry. Then, when he realized what he had allowed to happen, he became frightened. He looked at me, as if suddenly remembering the major, and then back at the boy, who was lying on his side with his neck and arms in exactly the positions into which they had fallen when McGruder had dumped him onto the table.

But then Buckley's face cleared. His confidence returned, and he motioned quickly to McGruder. "Go and find Dr. Mason, tell him that we need him," he said; and I wondered why I, too, had not thought of Mason.

CHAPTER *SEVEN*

WHEN DR. MASON came into the hut he did not examine the boy. Covered with the blankets, with the worst side of his face turned toward the wall, he did not seem to be in any danger. He might have been only asleep.

It was Russell that Mason attended to first. "What happened to this man?" he asked, taking his pulse and examining his eyes, which were still open. But Russell seemed to have gone blind. He did not blink when Mason waved his hand across his face.

"He was sick last night," Buckley replied impatiently, and he went to the table and looked down at the prisoner, as if Russell didn't matter.

Mason turned to me and repeated his question. I shrugged and said that, really, nothing had happened to him that hadn't happened to all of us.

"He's had a nervous breakdown," Mason said. "How long has he been lying here like this?"

I had to think for a moment. "About an hour," I said, "maybe more."

Mason muttered something under his breath, then he told Buckley to have Russell carried out of the hut. Buckley didn't seem to care and he gave the order to the sentries. Probably he was satisfied that Russell would be unable to talk for a long time. Dr. Mason gave him an injection. By the time the sen-

tries came in with a stretcher Russell's eyes had fallen slowly
shut. They rolled him off the cot and carried him out.

"Take him to the infirmary," Mason said, and wrote out a
note to be sent with him. "I'll be along when I can."

Then he turned to the table, without looking at any of us,
as if he knew now what he would find there; but when he stood
under the light and saw the boy's face for the first time—the
swollen temple, the now putrescent cheekbone, the blackened
lips—he raised his eyes and stared at each of us in turn, and
then he pulled down the blankets. When he saw the groin he
opened his bag quickly and called Finley to help him, as
though he dared not waste a second. Finley went to him
eagerly, suddenly revived by his presence, and the two of
them turned the boy on his back and set to work without
speaking to us or looking at us again.

My face had grown unaccountably hot when Mason
looked down at the boy's mutilated groin. But Mason was an
outsider. He did not understand how it had been in the room
when the knife had been in use. I felt a strong desire to explain
to him that it had been McGruder—and Nguyen, the boy's
protector—who were to blame; but Mason paid no attention
to me, and I said nothing. Finley would be able to tell him
what had really happened in the room. Later, I hoped, there
would be a time for that.

"He's alive, at least," Mason finally muttered, speaking
more to himself than to us, bending over the boy with a stethoscope on his chest while Finley cleaned the wounds on the
groin, removing the infected skin and bandaging what was
left. Finley's recovery puzzled me. He was all right now that
Mason had come. When he was told to give the boy a shot of
penicillin he did it with a steady hand, while before, when he

gave the injections he had trembled so hard that he couldn't hold the needle.

"We'll take him to the infirmary, too," Mason said when he had finished his examination. He straightened up and looked at Buckley. "He can't be kept here in this condition."

Then I thought that it was finally at an end, and I was grateful to Mason, for he had stopped it. But most of all I was grateful to the prisoner, for he had taken so much punishment that they dared do nothing more to him; he had survived, without giving in to Buckley. He had won, and his victory made me feel as if I too had won, and that I could rest.

Buckley, who had watched anxiously as long as the prisoner was being treated, stood up, now that he knew that he would not die, and shook his head.

"There's an interrogation going on here," he said, "and it isn't finished yet."

Mason summoned all of his disgust into one look, his face turned up under the light. "It's finished," he said. "I'm the medical officer of this godforsaken command, and the health of the inmates is my responsibility, not yours. We'll move him to the infirmary."

"This isn't one of your inmates," Buckley warned; "this is a Viet Cong prisoner of war."

"I don't care what he is!" Mason shouted. "He's going to die if he isn't properly cared for. Or do we execute prisoners now, too?"

Buckley smiled at Mason tolerantly and told him that the prisoner was not being executed. "Only interrogated," he said.

"It wasn't interrogation that put him in this condition."

"That was Nguyen's fault," Buckley said.

Mason seemed not to hear him. He turned to McGruder

and ordered him to bring a cot. "We'll use it for a stretcher," he said, and began to wrap the blankets around the boy's feet and neck, as if to move him. But McGruder stepped back against the wall. Mason looked up, frowning, and then he told Finley to do it instead.

"Put it down," Buckley ordered quietly when Finley lifted one end of the cot.

But Finley held it stubbornly, looking at Mason, waiting; and I saw, to my amazement, that even Finley was ready to fight.

"You exceed your authority, Lieutenant!" Mason cried. "As an Army doctor I have the rank of captain, and I'm telling you to stand aside and stop interfering! You run your camp. I don't tell you how. Don't try to tell me how to treat my patients."

It was the first time I had ever seen Mason lose his temper. But it did no good.

"It isn't my authority," Buckley replied in a quietly menacing voice. "I'm acting under the major's special orders. You know how things are here, Doctor. I'm surprised at you. You can remove the prisoner if you're willing to answer for it to the major, personally."

Mason watched him, and didn't say anything.

Buckley reached into his pocket for a cigarette. "They need doctors in worse places than Quai Dong."

Mason looked down at the boy. I could see that he was not going to risk it. For a moment he studied Buckley; then he glanced at me and seemed to reconsider, and to reach a conclusion.

"Very well," he said in a subdued voice, "we'll do what we can for him here. But I warn you, Buckley," he added, looking up, "that he can't take any more of the kind of punishment that's been administered to him. You'll kill him." He watched Buckley for a moment, then he said, "You think about answering for that."

Buckley assured him that he meant the prisoner no harm. "All we want is information."

It was clear that Mason and Buckley understood one another. Each knew what the major wanted, and how far he was prepared to go to get it. Finley sensed it too, and he lowered the cot without another word and retreated to the farthest corner of the room, as if he had lost all hope.

"Can he talk?" Buckley asked, edging ominously closer to the prisoner.

"No," Mason said flatly.

Buckley stopped and watched Mason's face. "He has to be able to talk," he said quietly, "before we can let him go."

Mason assumed his familiar expression of detachment. "That isn't my affair," he replied. "All I say is that he can't be touched again, not in any way. You'll kill him if you do."

Buckley agreed, and then he turned to me. "Kreuger," he said, "you'll have to carry on. You're the only one of us that can speak the language."

Now they were after me, even Mason, peering at me from under the light, trying to protect themselves. I asked Buckley what he wanted, and he said simply, "Interrogate him."

"I told you that I won't do that," I said.

Buckley shrugged, as if to say that in that case he knew of no alternative, now that Nguyen was gone, but one. McGruder was still in the room, standing next to Cowley by the tool crib, though it was there that Cowley had taken a hammer to kill him a few hours before. McGruder suspected nothing. His eyes were fixed contemptuously on Mason. Unable to stand the sight of an Army doctor treating a guerrilla, he had left the hut while the prisoner was being examined. When he came back he carried a hand generator. Now the black thing sat under his cot, squat and ugly, waiting. It looked like a field telephone, with double hand-cranks on either side and wires wrapped around its base. It would produce over a hundred volts if a strong man cranked it. McGruder could get at least that much out of it. He was waiting, with his bloodless device, more confident than ever that he would win in the end.

Mason had seen the generator and the wire leads. He knew what they were for, and what they would do to the boy, and yet it was obvious that he would not risk a fight to protect the prisoner even from that. He had seen how things were and he was keeping his head down, as he had advised me to do the day before. I did not hold it against him, for he had no way of knowing how bad it had been in the room. Only when a man had watched the interrogation for a day and a half did he realize that the simple act of watching made him a part of it. Even if you did not struggle on either side, you sank into the guilt of it, like quicksand.

I knew the alternatives too well to argue them any longer, even to myself. There was a deadly monotony in them that made their repetition hateful. We were alone, and had to find our own way out. "All right," I said, "I'll do what I can."

Buckley was relieved, and gave me such a look of good will that I wondered for a moment what he would have done if I had refused. Perhaps he would have given in. Like the rest of us, he faced an abyss where only McGruder could win.

But Nguyen and I had tried to stop him before. When Buckley was checked he became homicidal and did not care if the boy lived or died, since he had nothing more to gain from him. I was trapped; yet I knew that even inside the trap there were certain privileges. By keeping Buckley's hopes alive I gained time for the boy, and I gained control over what took place in the room. It was not much, but it was all that offered itself. Perhaps, if enough time passed, a way of escape would appear for all of us. One could never tell.

Temporarily, we waited. It was not until noon that Dr. Mason had the prisoner resting on the table with his eyes open. With the white bandages covering his cheek and groin he was less frightening to look at. Finley had been forced to leave his corner and come back into the light. He was holding a bottle of dextrose over him. The clear fluid dripped with a regular beat, like a pulse, through a tube that ran to a needle in the boy's ankle, nourishing him and restoring his strength in spite of himself. The room had come to resemble a hospital: intravenous tubes, empty bottles of plasma, packs of needles, bandages, and instruments, all lay in metal trays on the table and on my cot. A thin scent of Russell's vomit still hung in the air, but it had been nearly covered by a strong, cleansing odor of alcohol and disinfectant. It was a harsh, civilized smell, reassuring enough to allow me to approach the table.

Mason raised his eyes beneath the light and looked up at me over the boy's body. "What are you going to do?" he asked quietly.

"Talk to him," I said.

He shook his head, and glanced at Buckley, who stood against the far wall, watching us. "Stay out of it," he warned. "You know better than this."

I told him that all I wanted was to give the boy time. He might confess to me; or, if he remained stubborn, it would at least keep McGruder from getting hold of him. "There isn't any choice now," I said.

"Keep out of it," Mason repeated. "Let them have him, if that's what they want."

"You haven't seen what it's been like when they get their hands on him," I whispered. "Buckley will do anything to get a confession."

"I can see exactly what it was like," Mason said, pressing down a flap of tape over the bandage on the prisoner's abdomen. Finley looked sick. Mason glared up at me, his eyes narrowed with suspicion. "Use your head, Kreuger. You know what this camp is. Nobody gets killed, so nobody gets promoted. The major probably offered Buckley a recommendation for captain if he gets these guerrillas for him. Either of them would do anything to get a commendation from Saigon, if they think they have a chance."

I glanced at Buckley. Now I understood what he was after. Things made sense. We weren't sweating ourselves and sacrificing the boy for the hundred imaginary Americans. We were doing it for Lieutenant Buckley. But I told Mason that it didn't matter why Buckley and the major wanted their information. "The boy pays, in any case, if we don't help him."

"They can't let him die," Mason said, glaring at me as fiercely now, in his determination to stay clear, as he had glared at Buckley when he wanted to remove the prisoner to the infirmary. "He's their only source of information."

"If they're convinced that there's no hope, they'll kill him on the spot! You still don't know what it's been like in here."

172

"All the more reason to keep out of it, then," Mason said, lowering his eyes and going back to his work.

I glanced down at the boy's face, for one could look at it now without nausea, since the bandages hid the wounds. "I haven't hurt him," I whispered. "He'll talk to me."

Mason refused to say anything more. Buckley was becoming suspicious and moving back and forth around the door. Mason wanted only to avoid trouble. The Army did that to a man, even to a good man. But the room did something else. Mason did not yet understand that it was necessary to take some effective line of action. The only thing that I feared now was allowing things to run their natural course. I could see what that would be. McGruder and his machine would take my place with the boy. There was no one else to stand in his way. Then we would be forced—all of us, Mason and Finley as well as Buckley and myself—to watch an execution.

I began to put my questions to the boy, since there was nothing to be gained by explaining myself further to Mason. At first it went awkwardly, for I didn't know what to say to him. My voice sounded false. It was the role of the Inquisitor, and alien to me. But then I remembered how Nguyen had done it, and I tried to imitate him. I allowed the boy no rest, and demanded confession over and over, steadily, until my throat burned from it.

The prisoner stared up at me. His jaw was locked shut. Not even his eyes moved. In all the stillness of the room I was left alone with the sound of my own voice. The boy would not answer, and I was soon afraid to stop.

"Why did you want to go to Saigon?"

No answer.

"What is your sister's name?"

A fleeting expression in the black eyes; nothing more.

"You told Sergeant Nguyen that the dead soldier was North Vietnamese. Why was he on the road to Weichu?"

The boy gazed at me stubbornly and would not make a sound. He did not admit, even with a movement of his eyes, that he heard me. At the end of thirty minutes I had failed to draw a word out of him, or even a sign of recognition. The effort was immense. It seemed incredible that Nguyen could have kept it up for so long. But then the boy had answered him and they had developed a rhythm that sustained both of them. He was staring up at me now as Russell had stared at the wall, as if to defend himself with blindness. I used all that I could remember of Nguyen's questions. I used them as if they had some secret power of their own—questions of grenades, of medicines rolled in a blanket, of a sister in Saigon, the Weichu Road, the dead soldier, the dead family—I poured out the memory of meaningless facts as if I were reciting the mass of a religion in which I had no faith whatever. There was a feeling of unreality about all of it; it had nothing to do with the reason for the boy's being on the table under the light, or for any of us being in that room, waiting for him to speak. There was some other reason, some deeper answer that he could not give us; but I was unable to say what it was, and I repeated the words of grenades and roads and families that had died at Darlac as the simple repetition of a liturgy which, if repeated often enough, would suddenly explain everything to us. Cowley and Finley were watching me from the shadows along the wall. They seemed to fear that the interrogation was starting from the beginning again, inscribing only larger and more hopeless circles now and in the future, tomorrow, the next day, and the days that would follow, without end. But I paid no attention to their fear, for I could see that Buckley was satisfied now that he once again heard the meaningless sounds in which he placed all his hope.

But the effort was too much. I held on as long as I could, and then I had to stop. The cycle of absurd questions was unbearable. The heat of midday drove my throat to a hot thirst that even water could not slacken. My voice failed. I could not keep it up when I saw that the questions were useless. What was necessary was to enforce the deadening repetition of the answers on the prisoner. For that the knife was required, which was impossible. As it was, only I suffered, while the prisoner rested with Mason sponging the sweat off his face and listening to his chest. Then, too, my mind could not keep the questions in their proper order, and I was ashamed to have the prisoner see that I became confused. Once I saw a curl of scorn at the corners of his mouth. It was almost imperceptible; but it was there.

I changed my attack. The only hope was to abandon Nguyen's method and make the boy understand that I meant him no harm, that I was the only person standing between him and McGruder. The language freed me, for Buckley could not understand a word. I told the boy that I would not hurt him, that I did not care whether he confessed or not, but that he must say something so that the others could see that he understood me. Otherwise, I told him, they would use the electrical generator, in spite of what I might try to do to prevent it.

Still he was immovable. He might have been in a deep coma, with his eyes open, but Mason assured me that he was able to hear every word that I said. I emptied my mind over him again and again until the words began to lose their meaning to me, and I stumbled over them and got them backwards.

Mason continued his work. He checked the prisoner's eyes with a light and listened to his pulse. I could see the heart lifting faintly beneath the ribs with every beat; a gentle, but uncommonly visible thump against the wall of the chest, as if the space were too small and the thing was trying to free itself. Cowley was on his feet behind me, moving about uneasily; and Finley, who had fallen back into his self-defensive inertia, stood behind Mason, pale and withdrawn. He did not want to look at anything. I glanced over my shoulder once, and saw that Buckley and McGruder were watching me from across the room. That was all that mattered to me. Cowley and Finley would have to look out for themselves.

It was only after two hours of interrogation, when my voice was harsh and painful, that the prisoner finally closed his eyes and moved his lips. His voice was stronger now—Mason had done his job well—and we all heard him clearly, though I alone understood what he said.

He said simply that I was a fool. Then, opening his heavy eyes again, as if after an immense effort, he said that he would not utter another word until he died.

Mason looked up at me, frowning curiously. Buckley had jumped to his feet and was standing at my side, gripping my arm, looking rapidly from the boy to Mason and then to me. But the boy said nothing more. His mouth was closed; only his eyes looked up at us, black eyes, ringed and sunken, full of hate.

"What was it?" Buckley asked tensely, digging his fingers into my arm.

*176*

"Nothing," I said wearily.

"He said something! We all heard it!" Buckley snapped back at me. "What was it?"

"He's complaining of pain in his abdomen," I said.

"Well?" Buckley said, glaring at Mason.

Mason only shrugged. "It's possible," he said. "He'll be unconscious if I give him enough anesthetic to kill all the pain."

Buckley looked back at me; then he nodded slowly and returned to his cot. Again his eyes were distrustful. I wished that the boy had remained silent, for McGruder and Buckley had begun to whisper together, as if I had already failed.

I pressed the interrogation, afraid now to stop, though I no longer had any hope of success. The room was verging toward the same kind of madness out of which it had come when the boy had collapsed. It was necessary to convince him that he could trust me—that, for all our sakes, he had to trust me, if he was going to survive. But he was implacably stubborn. Nothing would move him. He fought me as if he hated me more than he had Nguyen. Neither promises of freedom, which would reunite him with his sister, nor my repeated word that I, too, hated Buckley and wanted nothing more than to defeat him, would make him look at me with anything but his unchanging face of hostility. In the back of my mind I recall having thought, quickly, that McGruder had been right: given the chance, the boy would have killed us all, Mason and Finley, myself, all of us together with Buckley and McGruder, without hesitation and without mercy, as if there were no difference between us. He seemed no longer to hear me, as if he had enclosed himself in some secret cell to which I had no access. Only his eyes were alive, following me from one side of the table to the other when I moved to ease the pain in my legs, or when Mason told me to get out of his way so he could do his work properly.

Eventually Mason found the wounds on the prisoner's back. He forced his hand under his body and when he drew it back it was smeared with blood. For some reason we had all been silent about those wounds, as though we had been ashamed. When we didn't tell him at once, it had become impossible for us to say anything. Even Finley, who should have shown Mason, had not said a word. Now Mason began to swear, furiously, and he turned the boy on his side. Then he made a thorough examination of the rest of his body and set to work cleaning and bandaging the wounds. He did the sterilizing and cutting and dressing himself. He did not call Finley, and Finley did not offer to help, for he did not want to be trusted anymore. No one wanted to be responsible.

The bad side of the prisoner's face was turned up to the light when Mason rolled him over on his side, but still he kept one eye on my face, following me, never letting me escape the gaze that came from behind the shadow of the swollen temple and the bandaged cheek, where I knew the bone lay open. The single eye followed me without a moment's release, accusing me, as if it could drive me out of the room by the power of its silent hate. At first I felt nothing; but finally, after I had stopped hearing the sound of my own voice intoning the ritual sounds of the alien language, it became unnerving, the single black eye, caught in the light, half hidden by the swollen cheek. There was no appeal against that look. I could not make him understand what I wanted. Probably he dreamed of killing me. All that I could do was promise him freedom, or threaten him; but the threat had no meaning on my lips, and there was no question of freedom. Already he was beyond our reach, waiting for McGruder, yet still fighting me, trying to get so far beyond human help that he would be able to die without interference.

Three o'clock came. The tin room poured the heat of the sun down upon us. My sides and back were soaked with sweat. The discomfort of it made me think of the work in the blazing heat on the beach, and reminded me that I was still a prisoner. It was not my business to be trying to break the boy's will, yet I had no choice. Everything in the room was fixed and immovable. Nothing could any longer be changed. All that remained now was to finish it. But still the boy's will resisted my demands that he confess. He struggled silently, with fanaticism. Mason sponged his face and neck; he changed the needles in his arms and ankles when the bottles ran dry; he listened through his stethoscope at his back, but the prisoner paid no attention to him. Nor did he turn his look of hate on McGruder or Buckley—only toward me, as if I, who wanted him to live, were his only enemy.

The air in the room was thick with heat and with the ring of silent anger. My body grew weak. Sweat trickled off my forehead and fell across my eyes. It was cooler than my skin and made me dream of the cool waters of the bay. My mind was numb, but I dared not stop. I held on, though no one helped me. I did not hate the boy—but I began to hate Mason, who had given up, and Cowley and Finley, who, like the prisoner, thought only of getting away.

At first the passing of time was slow and painful. But then it accelerated and blurred. One hardly felt it anymore. It was only the end that one awaited, even though no end was in sight. Eventually my mind grew dull and placid, and in its silence I ceased to hear anything but the sound of the interrogation, which seemed to come from far away. Then, when it seemed impossible for anything to stop us, there was a sharp knock at the door. I looked up, irritated by the intruding sound, fearing that something would happen to prevent me from beginning again. Buckley jumped up and opened the door. A blast of fresh air, furnace-hot, broke into the room, and with it came a flash of sunlight that splintered against the metal table and stabbed my eyes, awakening me. I heard the muffled sound of Buckley's voice. Then another voice that I did not know, whispering excitedly. Finally the door closed with a loud click, and Buckley was gone.

Once more we were alone, with the sun's light locked outside. McGruder and his machine sat on one side of the room, while Cowley prowled back and forth in front of the tool crib as if he had lost his mind. I began the interrogation with a sense of relief, but now my sides ached. My lungs were bruised and sore. The interruption had stopped me, and broken my strength. Added to the scent of disinfectant rose a smell of human sweat. I had not noticed it until the door had been opened and the fresh air had swept into the room to mingle with the stale odors of our mouths and bodies. The prisoner's armpits dripped across his chest. The metal surface of the table glistened moistly in the light. Everything was damp, sticky, reflecting the electric glare off wet flesh and from the edges of wet instruments, from scalpels and needles, wrenches, hammers; and in the middle of it there was nothing but my voice, reduced to a whisper, an incessant, meaningless whisper that went on out of simple weariness, without direction or hope. The corrugated walls drew closer together. The waves of heat rose up toward the light, blinding my eyes. My mouth was filled with the exhausted breath of my own lungs, stagnant, unwilling to give any further life to my body. In time I came to forget what it was that we had wanted, or why it need ever have begun. The process went on by an impulse of its own, impelled by a shapeless fear that something worse would take its place if it stopped. I did not know what the others felt. I seldom looked at them, for my eyes were heavy and wanted to close. Only the face of the prisoner had any strength left in it now. It was glued to mine with an unwavering look of hate. Finley was somewhere in the room, but he had retreated to the shadows again and was silent. He seemed hardly to exist. Cowley paced around me, watching the boy's face too, but with mounting impatience. Perhaps he was wearing out. I didn't know. I didn't care. For myself I no longer felt anything. Like the prisoner under the droning of the interrogation, I had grown too numb to feel pain; there was only a strong distaste in my mouth, and I welcomed it, for distaste was a cooler, less dangerous thing than anger. Gradually I was able to think clearly, though as if from a great distance. In time my mind became utterly detached from the objects in the room and I saw things as they really were, stripped of all illusion, with everyone in his proper place—and the alternatives rose before me in their stark clarity. The question, in itself, was simple, but our minds had confused it. It had always been within our power to finish everything. We should not plead. We needed only to convince the prisoner that it was necessary for him to cooperate, and I reached out, across a great distance, and picked up the knife. Nguyen had left it on the table, and Mason had wrapped it in a towel; yet I knew where to find it. My arm seemed dead. There was no feeling left in it, but my hand responded effortlessly to my will. My mind was calm. The motion was simple and easy, for I had only to tighten my fingers around the waiting handle and draw it along the surface of the table. The blade flashed in the light, then came down and touched the boy's chest, above the bandages, and slid along his pulsing ribs. They tightened. He felt the steel again, though it was flat side down, harmless. The expression in his eyes changed. A look of bewilderment came into his face. He seemed no longer to hate me. Then I saw a smear of blood spreading from under the edge of the knife, though there had been no sensation of cutting in the blade or in my hand.

Suddenly the silence of the room was shattered by a loud crash of metal behind me. I turned around and Mason shouted a warning, and then I saw Cowley's heavy face in the light.

"You dirty bastard!" he said.

He was backing along the far wall, glaring at me. McGruder was coming after him, but Cowley was keeping him off with a hammer that he swung in slow circles above his head. They passed near Finley, who ducked away and stood in a safe corner.

"Get out of my way!" Cowley shouted.

There was no weapon in the room—Buckley had seen to that—and McGruder had to move back.

"Put it down," he warned.

"Get away from the door!"

"Cowley!" Mason said sharply. "Are you out of your mind? Sit down!"

But Cowley shook his head, dumbly, and kept the hammer raised. He looked at McGruder, then at me, and at the knife, which had a little line of red along its edge.

*182*

"I'm getting out of this," he whispered, and lunged for the door.

McGruder jumped out of his way. Again there was the unbearable flash of sunlight when the door was thrown open. Cowley disappeared into it; he seemed to dissolve, as if the inhuman glare had swallowed him. But the door remained open, pouring its merciless light into the room, breaking against the bottles and instruments, blinding me.

McGruder ran out after Cowley. I saw him standing between the hut and the barbed wire, shouting at the top of his lungs. A voice, one of the guards, answered him. Nothing else was visible in that white heat. I wanted to shut the door and to go on now that I knew what had to be done, but when I went to the doorway I heard the guard call out again. This time it was a warning. I peered out of the hut to the left, against the sun, and saw Cowley. Already he was on the far side of the fences, walking deliberately away from the hut, toward the main gate and the sea. Ahead of him stretched two hundred yards of open ground. Behind him stood the guards with their carbines raised. Once more the cry of warning came, and then, like a hammer banged against the tin hut, a shot rang out. Cowley lurched forward. One leg buckled and he began to fall, but he straightened up and went on, as if nothing had happened. There was a perplexed silence. He was sixty yards from the gate now. One of the sentries looked back over his shoulder at McGruder. I looked too, and saw that McGruder was grinning, a trickle of sweat running from his temple to his jaw, where it soaked under the dirty collar of his shirt.

He allowed Cowley to walk for a moment longer. Then his smile hardened, and he said, "Stop him."

Instantly two more shots were fired behind me. I turned, and saw two guards standing by the corner of the hut. They looked frightened. When I turned back I saw that Cowley was now lying on his side, with his head in the dirt. He looked flat and small in the sunlight. The shooting, from beginning to end, had taken no more than one minute.

Mason came out of the doorway. When he saw Cowley he called for Finley to bring his medical kit, and then he ran through the opening in the barbed wire, past the sentries, and across the open ground. I watched Mason, who seemed to diminish, as if melting in the sunlight, until his size was as insignificant as Cowley's. Then he kneeled beside him and rolled him over.

Finley ran after him, and I closed my eyes, feeling the skin of my face burned and stretched by the heat, unable to look against that blinding light any longer.

Somewhere far off I heard one of the guards say, "He wouldn't stop," and another said, "We warned him, but he just kept walking."

They were frightened, but McGruder told them that they had only followed orders. "Don't worry," he said, "the crazy bastard was a convict," and they didn't try to explain themselves anymore.

The ringing sound was in the air again. It was the tin hut, blistering and cracking apart in the heat, or the distant sound of the sky itself, pouring its flame down on us. I opened my eyes and looked up at the sky. It closed us in with a burning dome that looked as hard as brass. My eyes were drawn by the white ball of fire in the west, but I did not close them; and then, with a sudden awakening, I felt the handle of the knife that my fingers still gripped.

*184*

McGruder walked slowly toward Mason and Finley. He had told two of the sentries to go with him, and two to stay at the fence. I glanced down. On the ground, by the open door, lay the hammer that Cowley had thrown away. My hand was stiff and aching. I had not realized that I was gripping the knife so hard. I unbent my fingers painfully and let the knife fall next to the hammer; and then I, too, began to walk toward Cowley, through the gap in the barbed wire fence and across the interminable distance that separated us, closer to the kneeling figures that gradually became life-size and real. I wanted to run. Everything came back. The sun blazed up into my eyes from the sand. It was incredible; three shots had rung out and vanished, as if nothing could hold them or call them back. There was nothing remaining but the senseless earth at our feet, the bronze sky, the flat, leaden sea—and trapped between them lay Cowley, with only our eyes to see him.

But he was not dead.

"They hit him in the back of the legs," Dr. Mason said, looking up at the guards, who bent over him with their rifle butts in the dirt. "His knees are shattered."

Mason and Finley had cut off Cowley's trousers and tied rubber tourniquets above his knees. A white powder had been poured like salt into the splintered wounds where the knee-caps had been shot away. All the while Cowley looked up at me, silently, as if he were looking back across a great distance. There was nothing to do but stare back at him. He looked unreal, lying in the dirt, bleeding. Only when he spoke did he show his pain, and he licked his lips.

"I told you I'd get away," he whispered.

"Give him morphine," Mason said, and Finley gave him the injection.

McGruder leaned over my shoulder and looked down at Cowley. "You're in for it now, soldier," he said.

"I don't give a damn," Cowley answered weakly, still keeping his eyes fixed upon me. "I wasn't going to see it start again . . . not for anything."

"Nothing was going to happen," I said, and I looked away from Cowley back across the flat ground to the hut. But now the hut, and not Cowley, looked small and unreal, with the diminutive sentries standing alone next to the fence. Everything there was moving, wavering uneasily in the heat. Nothing inside was visible; only the black hole of the open door. I watched it, feeling Cowley's eyes on my face, until they came with a stretcher for him.

"Don't bend his knees," Mason said.

Cowley groaned when they lifted him; but I did not watch how they did it, for now I saw a small figure, black against the sun's glare, coming toward us around the rows of trucks from the direction of the command post. It was Buckley, walking rapidly across the heat waves that lay in the distance like boiling water. Somehow, as I watched him, I imagined him sinking; yet when he reached us his boots were dry and covered with dust. He did not quite run, but when he looked at me his face was white and streaming with sweat.

"One hour ago," he said breathlessly, "the guerrillas ambushed a convoy ten miles from here. The major just got the word. They killed five Americans. One hour ago," he said, "in broad daylight!"

Buckley was angry, or frightened. He seemed not to see Cowley at all, nor did he appear to find it strange that all of us were standing in the open ground beyond the barbed wire.

*186*

No one said anything, except Dr. Mason, who told Finley to be careful to time the bleeding with the tourniquets on Cowley's legs. Buckley did not hear. He was staring at me as if he had been finally driven out of his mind.

"We've got to stop them now!" he exclaimed in a hoarse voice. "We have four hours of daylight left. This is the chance we've been asking for!"

The sentries stood up dutifully, though stupidly, as though they were ready to receive orders.

"Where did they hit us?" McGruder asked.

"On the main road a mile outside Tri Quang," Buckley answered, glaring at me as if he, too, thought that I was to blame. "They had it mined, and machine guns in place on both sides of the road. The convoy didn't have a chance. But they can't have gone far. Patrols are covering the area. We have a flight of copters coming in. All we have to know is where they're hiding their equipment. That's all we have to know!"

"They can go a long way in an hour," McGruder said.

"No," Buckley replied quickly, "they have too much equipment with them this time. They're going to be slow. If we're fast, we have a chance to get them."

"We'll move him to the infirmary," Mason said.

I heard Finley ask quietly if he would lose his legs.

"Most likely," Mason answered, and glanced up at Buckley. "Did you say there are helicopters coming in?"

Buckley looked down, and saw Cowley for the first time. "What happened to him?" he asked impatiently.

"He tried to make a break," McGruder said, "and we shot him."

"Are there helicopters?" Mason repeated angrily.

Buckley nodded. "A flight of six cobras is on its way from Bien Hao."

"All right," Mason said, "then we'll fly him out of here. He needs to get to a hospital as soon as possible."

Buckley stared down at Mason for a moment; then, as though he hadn't heard a word that he had said, he turned abruptly back to me.

"We want the information," he said, lowering his voice, as if to menace me, or to entice me. "We have to have it now. No more waiting. That kid in there has already cost us five dead men."

I glanced up at the hut and told Buckley that there was nothing to be done, unless he wanted to begin over with the interrogation. "He won't talk," I said, "and he's had a rest now. It will take a long time to wear him down again."

"Don't you understand what I'm saying to you?" Buckley asked furiously.

I watched him, understanding exactly what he was saying, and trying to think of some way to stop him. But it was too late.

"Kreuger, we'll get you out of this. For Christ's sake, you'll be a lieutenant again!" He was shouting, beside himself with rage, as if he could already hear the whirring of hovering helicopters asking for the target, which he could not give. "Damn it," he said, "he must have told you something in all this time!"

Cowley pulled himself painfully up on his elbows. I looked down at him accidentally and saw his face, straining to rise toward me. "You lousy bastard," he said.

Even Mason and Finley had gotten to their feet, staring

at me without a word. I wanted to make them understand that I had not sold out, that I had refused Buckley, that I had done everything to save the boy. But now Buckley had said it in their hearing. It was too late. The heat flared savagely off the ground between us. The air was on fire. I wanted to kill Buckley—but my hands were empty. The knife lay inside the fence. Only the guards were armed. I felt the others staring at my face. There was no way to defend myself. All that remained was hate—and I turned to Buckley, and watched his sweating face for a moment.

"Once," I said, "when Nguyen was questioning the prisoner, I heard him say that he was from the village of Bien Thieu."

Buckley grabbed my arm. "Are the supplies stored there?"

"I don't know," I said, watching the expression of eagerness that filled Buckley's red eyes, blinding him to everything but his desire. "All that he told Nguyen was that it was where his uncle lived. When Nguyen asked him if the guerrillas were from the village, he wouldn't answer."

Buckley pulled me away from the others and we headed for the command post. McGruder followed close behind us. Buckley did not ask me why I had not given him the information before, or why I had told him now. His face wore a look of great relief—almost of exultation. No doubt the major had come down on him hard. Now he did not think, he only hurried to tell his news and to present me as his savior and accomplice. They would radio the helicopters from Bien Hao, which would divert across the jungle to Bien Thieu. The patrols would converge. Now everything would take place by itself.

Once, before we turned the corner around the motor pool,

I looked back past the sweating face of McGruder and saw the small, slowly moving figures of the two sentries bearing Cowley away from the hut, farther from the open door with every step. He had made good his escape. Mason and Finley were walking alone back up to the shed. They, and not I, were the only survivors; but now I no longer cared.

CHAPTER *EIGHT*

O N C E we stepped inside the major's quarters every-thing changed. First of all it was the shock of cool air, for the air conditioner filtered out the heat and the smell of the earth and circulated only a clean, sterile atmosphere. Then, too, it was the color. Everything was white: the walls, the ceiling, the overhead lights, even the paint that covered the inside of the windows.

The staff sergeant with the neatly trimmed moustache stood up when we came in. Three or four other soldiers—clerks, really—sat at small wooden desks, typing. All that I could hear was the whir of the air vents and the clicking of the typewriter keys, punctuated now and then by the muted ring of their tiny bells.

"Bring the lieutenant a chair," Buckley said.

They seated me comfortably. Then Buckley and the ser-geant disappeared through a white door marked "KEEP OUT." I saw a long corridor with fluorescent tubes in the ceil-ing, and other rooms on both sides; then the door swung shut, and I was left alone with the silent clerks. On the blank wall behind the sergeant's desk there was a map divided into neatly colored areas of blue and green. Little pins and flags were stuck into it at regular intervals; and little squares, brown for the rest camp and black for the stockade, showed where each hut stood. The smallest brown square of all had a carefully let-tered number 34 on it. Only after I had searched the map thoroughly did I realize that that was supposed to be the machine shed.

I looked around, but no one was paying any attention to me. Still, I felt awkward. My stockade clothing was dirty and foul-smelling. There was no reason to sweat in that room, yet I was wet with it and stained from the sun. When I rubbed my face I felt a coarse stubble of beard. In the stockade there was a communal shower that we were allowed to use once a week, but I felt as though I had not been in it for a month.

For the moment nothing outside the white room was real to me. The simple act of sitting in their air-conditioned coolness made the attitude of the clerk-soldiers my own. I became ashamed of everything that had happened—not because it was brutal, but because it was dirty and foul-smelling. The glare of the sun, the blazing heat, the dust of the earth that settled indifferently on the barbed wire and the tin hut and the faces of men—none of it had any existence. From the point of view of the white room and of the men in it, what had taken place in the maintenance shed, and what had happened to Cowley, and to Nguyen, and to Russell, was unimaginable. I sat now in the real world, where the Army thought and made decisions— not where men died, and went mad. I let myself go. The well-painted room was as close to escape as I was going to get. But then I remembered that I had not escaped—that escape was impossible for me now. All that I had left was revenge.

Doors closed somewhere deep within the building. A telephone rang on one of the clerk's desks. He picked up the receiver, said, "Yes sir," listened, and then left the room with a pad and pencil tucked under his arm, as if to take dictation.

His female briskness offended me. Suddenly I was once again an outsider. I could not imitate them, and they began to disgust me. Their mindless work was like a dream, beyond my reach. I was the convict at whom they contrived not to look if they could help it. No doubt I stank, and disgusted them. Behind their indifferent faces they must have been eager for me to leave. But soon enough, I thought, they would see what the violence of the real world was like, when Lieutenant Buckley burst back into the room, red-faced and screaming for Kreuger.

For the moment the surface of things remained unruffled. Everything was efficiency and indolence. The clerks did their work without understanding what they were a part of, or what was about to happen. All of my hate for the Army revived as I watched them. I sat unobserved in their clean room, where any intrusion, either of passion or of logic, seemed impossible, and waited. Something was ticking—the typewriters or the whirring blades of the fans above the ceiling, building up to the inevitable explosion. I wanted to begin laughing, though I was not amused.

It was not likely that anyone would be killed. All that the patrols would find would be the women and children, for the farmers would still be in their rice paddies. Maybe empty huts, full of dung, with a few chickens; or, if Bien Thieu happened to be a rich village, some pigs. The columns of infantry would pull back, disgusted. The cobra pilots would return to Bien Hao without a rocket fired. They would tell the story tonight in Saigon bars, swearing or chuckling about Quai Dong. And the major would have no one to come down on but Buckley.

I looked up at the ceiling, toward the whirring sound of the invisible blades. They must have been on the other side of the acoustic tile. It was a very good office. But it was the door marked "KEEP OUT" that interested me most. It didn't move. Behind it, somewhere, Buckley was with the major. I tried to picture him giving his information. Probably he was quiet and effective, as a staff officer should be. That would end soon enough. All that I wanted now was to see him come back into the room, looking for me, and for his empty revenge. Then my days could go on as they had before, from four-thirty in the morning until sunset, digging mindlessly on the beach. They could do what they wanted with me. I wouldn't care. Buckley was going to remain a lieutenant.

But they didn't let me stay to see it. The staff sergeant came back and told me that I could go.

"Lieutenant Buckley wants you to wait with the prisoner," he said, and slipped noiselessly back behind his desk.

I stood up and left the room without a word. It didn't matter whether I was there to see it or not. I would know when it happened, and it would be better to wait with Dr. Mason and with the boy than with the silent clerks. It would be possible to explain to Mason and to make him understand that I had not given in to Buckley.

From the headquarters to the machine shop was a distance of three hundred yards. The afternoon sun was blazing across every foot of it. Only now it was oblique, coming out of the west. The sky was still metallic and hot, but simmering, with the worst of the heat past. Small shadows were coming out from under rocks and the sweltering sides of huts. Soon, when the sun touched the hills, the shadows would stretch all the way to the bay and the air would begin to cool. Already the evening breeze was stirring from the sea and bringing the salt smell of the rotting seaweed that the tide left on the beach, spawning flies in the sun's heat until the tide took it back to sea. Eventually the sun itself would collapse, falling in a misshapen red ball through the green bands of evening sky over the distant jungles, and with a last flash of enfeebled fire it would enlarge and vanish, and the earth would grow cool.

I did not mind the heat, now that the worst was over. It was the thought of beginning again that was unbearable, or of going on forever. But now there would be no beginning again. I had seen to that. I looked over the deserted camp and toward the empty bay. All that I saw were the shimmering rooftops and the windowless tin walls. There was no living thing in sight. Only myself. A man could have been in the heart of a desert and have been no more alone. I stood for a moment and calmly watched that profound emptiness. There had been nothing outside the hut that could have helped us. Only a handful of men knew of our existence, and they cared for nothing but their own advantage. We had been cut off from all hope, except that which we could make for ourselves. I looked at the rings of barbed wire and at the blind huts. Men, convicts and soldiers together, lived in them with their eyes fixed on the ground, waiting for their salvation, yet doing nothing to bring it. I knew that I had done all that a man could at Quai Dong, and I was satisfied.

I walked on alone until I reached the row of trucks at the motor pool. Suddenly I saw Finley appear from between two nearby huts. He was running, head down, with empty bottles in both hands.

I called to him and asked him where he was going, and he shouted back that he was on his way to the infirmary.

"What for?"

He looked at me distractedly and said something that I could not make out. Then he ran on, as though he was never coming back. I headed for the hut. The sentries were still posted, but they didn't challenge me. They seemed too exhausted to stand up, and sat on the ground with their backs against the wall and their carbines against their knees.

I opened the door and went in. Everything in the room was still at furnace heat, in spite of the cooling air outside. I left the door open, for the walk had filled my lungs with fresh air, which made the stench of sweat and the smell of disinfectants strike my senses hard. I said hello to Mason and sank down on the cot nearest the door, where I could feel the outside air. The boy still lay on the table under the light. I closed my eyes. There was nothing to do but wait.

But Mason got up and slammed the door shut. "You left him alone!" he shouted.

I looked up. Mason's face was nearly unrecognizable. "Who?" I asked.

"You left the prisoner alone," he repeated. "None of the rest of us knew!"

"What are you talking about?"

"He's dead," Mason said.

I sat up and looked quickly at the table. There were dark stains on the dirt under it, on the far side nearest the wall. I got away from Mason as soon as I was on my feet, for he looked suddenly menacing; and I saw that the opposite side of the table, to the left of the boy, away from the door, was covered with a great pool of blood. There was so much of it that it did not look like blood at all. It was dried and black where it had soaked into the dirt floor.

"What happened?" I asked, edging closer under the light until I was able to see the boy's face, which had fallen to the left, as if he had watched the pool of blood as it grew. The eyes were only half shut, but the skin, under the light, was pale and glistening.

"He used one of the scalpels," Mason said. He sounded tired now, and moved away from the door, where he had stood as if he would keep me from leaving the room. "The wrist of the left hand was cut to the bone. See for yourself."

I didn't look. I had seen bloodless bodies before, but they had been covered with dust or mud. The boy lay on the table under the electric bulb, which made him look white and unprepared for death.

"He knew exactly where to find the artery," Mason said. "We were gone for fifteen minutes. When we came back he was already dead." He looked at the body for a moment, then he added: "I thought someone was here with him. The scalpels were there in that pan."

The boy's face looked so unchanged that I asked Mason if he was sure that he was dead.

"Don't be a fool! We gave him transfusions, but he'd been without a pulse for probably ten minutes by the time we came back from helping Cowley. There," he added matter-of-factly, "you can see where the plasma drained off into his tissue. There wasn't any circulation left to carry it. The arteries had collapsed and we couldn't get the needles in properly." He turned the boy's wrists over. "It was hopeless, but of course we had to try," he said, and turned the hand over again, as if to hide it.

Mason seemed to blame himself. Every piece of cloth in the room had been used in a futile effort to mop up the blood. A pile of them lay in a corner, looking like a thick clot. Even the newspaper that he had given me the day before, and which I had thrown away in the night, had been used. It lay crumpled on the floor beneath the table, stained dark red and stiffening now in the heat.

"The guards were just outside the door," I said. "I can't understand how he could have done it without them hearing."

"They were watching Cowley, like the rest of us," Mason replied. He shrugged. "A scalpel doesn't make much noise. All he had to do was keep himself from crying out when he cut."

I walked around the table. One of the boy's thin hands lay on his naked thigh. It was perfectly still, though in every other way it looked all right, since the severed palm was turned down. Only some streaks of dried blood, turning brown, showed on the flesh of the leg.

"Kreuger," Mason said, watching me narrowly from across the table, "Finley told me that the interpreter, Nguyen, knew that the boy was suicidal. Did you know it too?"

Mason spoke with great effort. He seemed exhausted, but determined to go on. There was nothing for me to say. I was too tired to argue with him. I told him that I had known, but that we had rushed out after Cowley, all of us, and that no one had been thinking about the boy. "After all," I said, "Cowley was my friend."

Mason watched me for a moment; then he rubbed his face slowly with both hands and sat down wearily on my cot. "There's nothing to be done now, in any case," he said. But after a moment he looked up. "Buckley had what he wanted. The interrogation was over. The kid had nothing more to fear, but I suppose that was why he killed himself."

"What do you mean?"

"Don't pretend to be such a fool, Kreuger! I mean that he informed on his own people!"

I looked at the boy's face. The bandages seemed useless

and out of place on it now. "Isn't there anything we can cover him with?" I asked.

Mason shrugged. "You can use a blanket, I suppose, if you think it matters. They'll come for him in a little while."

Mostly it was the blood that I wanted to cover. I had never seen so much before. "Do you mind if I open the door?" I asked. "It's cooler outside now."

Mason said that he didn't care, one way or another, but when I opened the door the fresh air seemed to revive him and to rekindle his anger.

"Nothing matters to you, does it? The kid is dead, and mostly it's your fault, and you don't give a damn!"

I didn't want to have trouble with Mason. I didn't even want to explain things to him anymore. Above all else now, I didn't want trouble with anyone. Only Buckley. "There's nothing that can be done about it now," I said. "I wish he were alive, if that's what you mean."

"All right," Mason said, leaning back. "Forget it. I guess it was no one's fault. I left him alone too."

I was sorry that I had come back to the hut, and I asked him if Cowley would be all right, wanting the time to pass.

Mason said that he didn't know. "He'll never walk normally again, that's certain. It looks like no one will get out of this in one piece."

I asked him if he had a cigarette.

"No," he said.

Then he looked up at me, speaking with suppressed anger in his voice. "You gave Buckley his promotion, you know. I wish you hadn't done that."

I got up and stood in the open doorway. "I didn't give Buckley a thing."

"Hell, man, we all heard you!"

"The boy didn't tell me a damn thing and he was never going to," I said quietly, looking across the deserted camp. "The major was on Buckley's back. He and McGruder were going to get the information they needed out of the kid if they had to kill him to do it. All I did was get them out of here to buy time for the rest of us."

"But the boy is dead anyway," Mason said bitterly.

I could see the sun-baked ground outside the fence, and I didn't say anything for a minute. "That wasn't my fault."

"What about Bien Thieu?"

I turned around and looked down at Mason. "As far as I know there's nothing there."

Mason examined his hands for a moment. Then, in spite of the presence of the dead boy, he almost smiled, and said, "Well, I'll be damned."

"So Buckley's finished," I said. "He missed his chance at the guerrillas, and now the kid has escaped. There's nothing more he can do."

Mason shook his head. "He's going to come down on you."

"I don't give a damn what Buckley does," I said, feeling the heat prickling my face and hands.

Mason got up and drew one of the blankets off the cot and laid it gently over the boy's body. Only his face and toes were visible, thrusting up under it. Then Mason offered me a cigarette. We smoked together, with the fresh air from the open doorway moving slowly into the room.

"You're a fool, you know," he said, but he wasn't angry anymore.

Finley came back. He glanced distrustfully at me from the door, but when he saw that Mason was smoking with me he came in. He sat down across from us with his hands hanging lifelessly on his knees, without looking at the light or the table.

Mason asked him how Cowley was going.

"Okay," Finley said. "They've got him in splints now."

I thought about Cowley for a minute and tried to picture his face. He wouldn't do hard labor again.

"What will happen to him?" I asked.

Mason shrugged, and said that he'd wind up in a Stateside hospital. "They don't have any use for a cripple out here," he said.

I got up and crossed the room, keeping away from the dead body, and picked up a can of coffee that was sitting on the floor. But it was empty. McGruder had finished it.

"There's some cold meat next to my bag," Mason said, "if you feel like eating."

"I'm not hungry," I replied, and went back to my cot.

We kept the death wake over the prisoner. The body lay on the table in the center of the room, high up under the light, as if nothing had happened to it since McGruder had thrown the boy down there hours before. Mason was very quiet now. Only Finley was on his feet and moving about; he couldn't sit still, and kept wiping his face with his hand to stop the sweat from getting into his eyes. But his hand was dirty, and he streaked the dirt across his forehead. I supposed we all looked the same. Nothing else moved, except that now and then we could hear a guard stir restlessly outside the fence, or the sound of the tin cracking overhead. A fly found its way in through the open door. It circled the room for a while and then settled on the blanket over the boy's face.

We waited. I began to feel sick to my stomach. I dreaded

what was coming, though I tried not to think about it. Not so much because of what they would do to me—I was almost indifferent to that—but because, now that the boy was dead, I had no way to defend myself. I hated to see it made so easy for them.

"Let me have a drink," I said.

Mason filled his cup with warm water and handed it to me. "Are you all right?" he asked, looking at my face.

"It's the heat," I said. "I'm okay."

He shifted closer to me. "Listen, you use your head when Buckley comes back. He can't blame you because he didn't find anything in that village. All you did was tell him what the prisoner had already told Nguyen. He has no way to argue with you about that now, since the kid is dead."

"No," I said.

Mason leaned back, nodding. "There's nothing he can do to you. Only Finley and I know that you lied to him, and we aren't going to tell Buckley anything that we don't have to."

"I am," I said.

Mason looked at me, and frowned. "Why, for Christ's sake?"

"It's something between Buckley and me," I said. "I want him to know."

"But there's no reason for it!"

"If I keep quiet, Buckley only made a mistake. But if I tell them what I did, and keep on telling it no matter where they send me, he made a fool out of himself. He's finished. I don't care what happens after that."

"You're only making trouble for yourself," Mason said, shaking his head.

"Okay, it's none of your business, so keep out of it."

"You'll make trouble for the rest of us, too."

"Goddamit, Mason, that kid was killed in here."

"It wasn't only Buckley who killed him," he replied.

I got up and walked toward the light without looking at Mason. "Buckley brought us in here," I said. "None of it would have happened if he'd left us all alone."

"All right."

"If we keep our mouths shut now, he gets what he wanted. But he's not going to profit by this—not if I have to go to hell to prevent it."

"All right," Mason said, "sit down."

I went back to my cot and leaned against the wall. There was no point in talking to Mason anymore. He was going to look out for himself. "I know how to take care of Buckley," I said. "I'm the only victim he's got left, and there's nothing he can get out of me."

Mason was silent for a long time, then he said, "You take my advice. The boy is dead. Nothing matters to him now. You play along with Buckley and nothing will happen. You're sticking your neck way out."

"I know what I'm doing."

"Okay," Mason answered, "but keep us out of it."

I wondered why he didn't go back to his infirmary to do what he could for Cowley, now that there was nothing that he could do for the boy. But instead he remained in the hut. Probably, I thought, he wanted to see it when they came for me, in spite of what he said; or maybe he was too tired to move yet. I didn't care, one way or another. Mason might be good to have around when it happened.

"You know," he said speculatively, "they'll have you up for aiding the enemy again, only this time they're going to throw the book at you." Then he added wryly: "You won't have much of a reputation as an interpreter after this."

I put my head back against the hot wall and closed my eyes. What Mason had said struck me as funny and I wanted to laugh, but my face was too tired to do it.

Finley wanted to know what we were talking about. "What's the matter with him?" he asked, looking at me.

His voice was thin and piping. I didn't want to have to listen to Mason telling him, but he did it anyway. After that I avoided Finley's eyes. Somehow it made me uneasy to see a look of comradeship on his face. Still, it was in the room. Even the prisoner seemed to be a part of it now.

"Listen!" Mason said, and turned to look out the door.

But I had been hearing it for several minutes already: a distant hum of engines was on the air—helicopters. The flight of cobras was on its way home. Through the open door I could see a narrow strip of the distant sea. Both the water and the sky were fading to green now. Finally four tiny specks crawled into view over the bay, moving slowly, just off the water, then disappeared toward the coast, avoiding the jungle.

"That must be the flight from Bien Hao," Mason said quietly, and looked at me.

Mason began to irritate me. He sounded as if he were about to witness an execution. I nodded, and said nothing. It was the flight from Bien Hao, two aircraft short.

Then, out of the distant hum, one sound grew nearer. Soon we could hear an engine hovering above the camp.

"It's landing behind the C.O.'s," Finley said, standing in the doorway, squinting, blocking my view of the limitless sea, which seemed very important to me now.

Mason was on his feet, moving impatiently back from the door to the table with his hands in his pockets. Every time he turned around at the table he looked at the boy, then down at me. I sat on my cot silently and waited.

Presently there was a roar, followed by a loud whirring sound, which diminished swiftly, lifting away from us. Finley ran out to the fence with his hands shielding his eyes, then came back. "It's taken off!" he said. In a few minutes I saw it across the bay, racing to catch up with the others. That was five. Then everything was silent once more, except for the ticking of the hut, cooling under the waning sun.

A quarter of an hour passed, and no one came. My patience began to weaken, and I asked Mason for another cigarette. Everything considered, the waiting was the worst part of it.

"You stay clear of this," I said.

Finally we heard a familiar voice, and the sounds of the guards scrambling to their feet; and then, simultaneously with the crunch of heavy footsteps, Buckley's face appeared in the doorway, staring down at us. Mason got up instantly, with his hands thrust angrily into his pockets, and stood in front of me, full of resistance. I didn't move, and hardly looked up, for McGruder was peering in at me over Buckley's shoulder.

"Is everything all right here?" Buckley asked, looking about the room casually.

Mason seemed puzzled by the question for a moment. He had seen the look on McGruder's face, and expected the worst. He kept in front of me, as if to shield me. "The prisoner is dead," he said.

Buckley glanced at the table, a little surprised. "How did it happen?"

"He slashed his wrist with a scalpel when we were outside with Cowley," Mason answered, watching him angrily. "He was dead when we came back."

Buckley neither looked at the boy nor at me. All that he said was that he should be moved, if he was dead, and then he glanced around the room. "We can clear everything out of here now," he said. "None of it will be needed anymore."

Mason looked at him as though he would say something more; but McGruder came in to supervise the removal of the equipment, and he brought the sentries with him. They stacked their rifles against the fence and began to fold up the cots and pack Mason's things away. The boxes and the tin cans were taken outside, one by one, until the room was nearly empty.

Mason stood under the light, turning this way and that, moving back. "Be careful!" he shouted when one of the guards upset a tray full of plasma bottles. The sudden commotion seemed to confuse him, and he forgot about me. But then even my cot was taken, and I was forced to stand up. Buckley took one last look around the room, his hands resting lightly on his hips. Only when he was finished did he look at me.

"Sergeant McGruder," he said, "when you've secured the hut bring Lieutenant Kreuger to the major's quarters."

"Yes sir," McGruder answered, and glanced at me.

Buckley turned away and left the hut without another word and without a sign of anger. I saw him stop by the fence to light a cigarette; then he threw the match away, looked up at the sky, took the cigarette out of his mouth, and walked on.

There had not been time to say anything. One of the guards moved past me with a cot over his shoulder. He didn't see me, and I had to get out of the way. Mason was watching me. There was a strange look of uncertainty on his face. I looked at him until he turned away and told the guards to be careful. Then he began to pack away his surgical instruments. Finally nothing remained in the room but the table, with the dark stains in the dirt under it, and the prisoner's body. The guards stared at it as they moved in and out of the hut, but no one said anything. Finley stood by the door, weary, yet strangely reluctant to leave. When everything was finished, Mason picked up his bag, which was the only thing that the guards hadn't taken with them, and came to the door. Still he seemed unwilling to go. He glared at McGruder, who was the only one of us who looked pleased with the way things had turned out.

"Come on, Lieutenant," McGruder said.

But Mason put his arm across the doorway. "Wait a minute," he said quietly. "I want to know what happened at Bien Thieu."

McGruder shrugged. "Nobody's sure," he said.

"Tell us about it," Mason insisted, his eyes hard now, looking at McGruder, then at me.

"It was a turkey shoot," McGruder replied.

"But there wasn't anything in Bien Thieu," I said.

"What happened, Sergeant?" Mason asked, still holding his arm across the open doorway.

McGruder glanced at me. "I wasn't there," he answered, "so I can't say. All I know is our patrols drew fire when they got near the village, and they called down the cobras. One of them was hit, but the rest flattened the place with rockets. When it was over our guys went in and cleaned it up. We heard it on the radio," he said, and added, "there was *some*-thing at Bien Thieu."

Mason moved away from the door and walked to the light. "So Buckley got his guerrillas," he said. "I wish you hadn't done that, Kreuger."

"There was nothing at Bien Thieu," I said. "It was nothing but a name, a guess!"

Mason moved to the table. He was swearing quietly to himself and wouldn't listen to me. "How many were killed?" he asked.

"One of the cobras, like I said," McGruder replied. "I don't know if the crew got out of it or not."

"I mean in the village!" Mason shouted, turning around.

McGruder blinked. "How should I know? If there were guerrillas in there, we got 'em. Somebody was shooting at us. Anyway, Lieutenant Buckley said it was the outfit we were after."

Mason looked down at the prisoner, and didn't say anything.

"It was an accident!" I said. "The kid never mentioned Bien Thieu. How could any of us have known?"

Mason still refused to say a word. Suddenly I saw Finley slip silently away, escaping. He turned out through the fence and began to run, head down. I watched him, but once I had looked at the doorway it was difficult to look back. The sunlight was still hard and glaring. The rifles that the guards had left against the barbed wire gleamed black with oil. My head and body ached with fatigue.

"Kreuger," Mason said very softly, standing directly behind me, "you knew that this would happen."

"Don't be an ass," I said, looking back, "I couldn't have known."

He started to say something, but suddenly he closed his

eyes and laughed. "A column of G.I.'s would draw fire from any village in the district! Of course you knew, you bastard. It was the only way to get yourself out of this."

McGruder was looking at Mason as if he thought he had gone crazy. He was afraid of him and moved behind me to the door. "Let's go," he said.

"Not yet!" Mason shouted, and locked his fingers around my arm. "Not until I find out what the lieutenant is going to do."

"Exactly what I told you. Nothing has changed."

"Everything has changed! I don't give a damn about Buckley. He has what he wanted. So does the major. I want to know what you're going to do about the boy."

"Let go of my arm."

"Don't you understand that you can't get at Buckley now? He's won!"

"Come on, Lieutenant," McGruder said.

Mason pulled me after him and went back to the table and stood under the light. "What are you going to do about it?" he asked.

"I know how to handle Buckley," I said.

Mason bent forward. He looked tired, and he let go of my arm. Then he pulled the blanket away from the boy's head and shoulders. The face was very gray now. The skin was pulled tight. It gleamed under the light, but it was no longer moist. Only the bandages had a little red on them, where his cheek had bled the day before—or maybe it had been during the night, I couldn't remember anymore.

"Go back to the stockade," Mason said very quietly.

"They'll send me back when I tell them what happened in here," I said. "I'm still going to deal with Buckley."

Mason turned around. "All right," he said, and he looked at me for a moment; then he nodded slowly, as if he was very tired and finally believed me, and said, "Good luck."

McGruder was waiting outside at the fences. "Come on," he said, almost pleadingly. "I've got to detail someone to move this body."

I followed McGruder out into the daylight, where the long afternoon shadows were growing around the hut. Before us there was a sudden open expanse of earth. There were no more walls, no fences, except those in the distance, and beyond them stretched the beach and the open sea. Finally there was only the sky.

"You're going to tell them?" Mason called after us when we were beyond the barbed wire fence.

"Yes!" I answered.

He raised his hand then and stood in the sunlight next to the doorway. Behind him, in the darkness of the hut, I could see the body of the boy. It lay under the electric light, which made it strange to see from the sunlight in which we stood. It looked unreal, framed by the doorway like a picture, and, like a picture, it was suddenly very remote.

I turned away and hurried after McGruder. I didn't want to think about the room anymore. The red earth underfoot reassured me. McGruder was kicking up little clouds of dust from under his boots. I followed him, watching his broad back and his arms swinging as he walked around the corner of the motor pool, where the trucks at last cut us off from Mason's view. We turned toward the major's quarters. Then I saw the distant flag on the staff, stirring slightly in the cool evening breeze. The darkness of the room was behind me, out of sight. All that remained to remind me of what it had been like was the mild heat of the evening sun and the hot sides of metal huts. Ahead there was only the cool night, when I could sleep and forget.

We reached the wooden porch. McGruder glanced over his shoulder, as if to make sure that I was still there, and we went up the steps into the shade and opened the door. From the major's porch I could see all the way to the beach; and before I went in I looked back at the distant stockade. Convicts were still scraping the hull of the LST. They were on the port side now. I saw the orderly rows of khaki tents, the guard towers, the spotlights, and the barbed wire. Everything seemed unchanged; the only difference was that I was now standing on the major's porch, instead of on the beach.

The heat was getting in around me, and one of the clerks shouted, "Shut the door!" I let go of the handle and went into the coolness of the room. The door closed itself behind me. McGruder was already sitting in a chair with wooden arms, wiping his face.

"He'll take care of you now," he said, and nodded to the staff sergeant, who got up from behind his desk.

He came to me and said that his name was Morris. I told him that mine was Kreuger, and he said, "Yes sir, I know." Then he led me through the door marked "KEEP OUT" and down the long corridor, under the rows of fluorescent lights, past the doors of other rooms on the left and the right. We stopped in front of the last one. Morris asked me to wait, and went in and closed the door behind him.

The sound of the typewriters came faintly from the other end of the building. Behind a wall, close by, a radio was picking up a lot of static. It was a long wait. There was nothing to do but look at the walls and listen. I wished that I had a cigarette. The heat of the walk up from the machine shed had made me sweat, and now I was chilled in the cold air. I thought of Mason. I wondered if he was still in the sun's heat outside the hut, waiting with the boy; and it was only then that I realized that I had not escaped at all, in spite of all that I had been through—for now I would eat in the officers' mess, and three times a day I would find Mason's face somewhere in the room, waiting for me to look at him.

I waited until they came for me, wanting badly to laugh, if laughter had been possible at the end of that corridor. When the door finally opened it was Buckley who came out. He was smiling, and he took me by the arm and said that he had been instructed to show me to my new quarters in the officers' billet. "Is there anything that I can get for you?" he asked.

"First of all, I'd like a clean uniform," I said.